No Time to Say Goodbye

No Time to Say Goodbye

Children's Stories
of Kuper Island Residential School

Sylvia Olsen with Rita Morris and Ann Sam

sononis PRESS
WINLAW, BRITISH COLUMBIA

NATIONAL LIBRARY OF CANADA CATALOGUING IN PUBLICATION DATA
Olsen, Sylvia, 1955-
    No time to say goodbye

    ISBN 1-55039-121-6

    I. Title.
PS8579.L728N6 2001   jC813'.6   C2001-911140-1   PZ7.O577No 2001

First Printing: September 2001
Second Printing: November 2005
Third Printing: May 2011
Fourth Printing: March 2016
Fifth Printing: October 2016

Sono Nis Press most gratefully acknowledges support for our publishing program provided by the Government of Canada and the Canada Council for the Arts, and by the Province of British Columbia through the British Columbia Arts Council and the Book Publishing Tax Credit, Ministry of Provincial Revenue.

The authors would like to thank the Aboriginal Healing Foundation for financial assistance with the research of this book.
All royalties from the sale of *No Time to Say Goodbye* support Indigenous Youth Programs.

Edited by Ann Featherstone, Freda Nobbs and Dawn Loewen
Map by Patrice Snopkowski
Archival photos: page 37 (top) BC Archives # C-06115
                page 37 (bottom) courtesy of the authors
                page 151 BC Archives # D-05809

Published by
Sono Nis Press
Box 160
Winlaw, BC V0G 2J0
1-800-370-5228

Distributed in the U.S. by
Orca Book Publishers
Box 468
Custer, WA 98240-0468
1-800-210-5277

books@sononis.com   www.sononis.com

Printed on acid-free paper that is forest friendly
 (100% post-consumer recycled paper) and has
been processed chlorine free.

Printed and bound in Canada by Houghton Boston Printing.

The Canada Council | Le Conseil des Arts
for the Arts | du Canada

Funded by the
Government
of Canada | Canadä

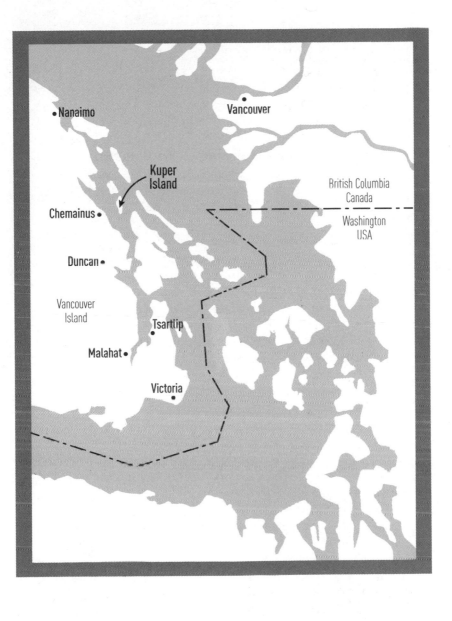

Preface

Over almost a century, hundreds of First Nations children were taken from their homes to live at Kuper Island Residential School. The school was isolated on a small island, one of the Gulf Islands between Vancouver Island and the British Columbia mainland. Accessible only by private boat until the 1960s, the island cut off the children from their families and communities. Some children stayed a short time, while most lived at the school for five to ten years, returning home only for summer and, sometimes, Christmas holidays.

Kuper Island Residential School was one of many similar schools across Canada, funded by the Canadian government and operated by the churches. The Kuper Island school opened in the late nineteenth century and finally closed in 1978.

Approximately twenty percent of all First Nations children living on reserves in Canada were taken to the residential schools. Some went willingly, with their parents' consent. For others, there was often no clear reason why they were selected to attend the schools.

The experiences at the residential schools have left many deep and lasting scars on First Nations individuals, families and communities. Over the past decade many former students have begun to tell their stories and call the Canadian government and churches into account for their participation in running the schools. Living with the residential school experiences and telling the stories is often difficult and painful, and First Nations people across Canada are now working on healing the wounds left by the schools.

No Time to Say Goodbye is a fictional account of the lives of five children taken to Kuper Island from Tsartlip Day School, on southern Vancouver Island, in the 1950s. The experiences of these children—Thomas, Wilson, Joey, Monica and Nelson—have been recreated from stories collected from former students of Kuper Island Residential School. None of the children are real and any resemblance to real persons is unintended. However, many of the experiences have been shared by thousands of First Nations students throughout Canada.

Six former students from Kuper Island Residential School read and edited *No Time to Say Goodbye* many times before approving the book. The book was written to honour them and all the other First Nations people who experienced the residential schools.

The former students hope that young people for many generations will learn about this neglected but important part of history through reading this book.

Although I wrote *No Time to Say Goodbye*, I was only one of many people who shared in the project. The six former students of Kuper Island Residential School whose stories inspired this work and who acted as story editors—Ralph Bartleman, Clyde Jack, Sandy Morris, Laura Olsen, Rose Smith and Simon Smith—generously offered their memories and their comments about their experiences. Their observations and wisdom guided my writing throughout. Rita Morris and Ann Sam recorded their memories and helped revise the resulting stories, showing both sensitivity and persistence. The Aboriginal Healing Foundation saw the importance of funding this project on behalf of those who attended residential schools and their children and grandchildren. Carl Olsen and Tsartlip First Nation sponsored the project. Ron Martin, Wayne Kiers and Dorothy Paul read the early drafts and contributed worthwhile suggestions and observations. Scott Henthorn and Connie Paul produced the wonderful map and artwork. Publisher Diane Morriss had the vision and courage to publish the stories. My children, Adam, Joni, Heather and Joaquim, listened to the stories and gave me constant support. Yetsa, my granddaughter, Diane, my sister-in-law for life, and Laura are my inspiration, and Tom is my friend and source of encouragement. Thank you all.

I also thank all the former students of Kuper Island who have shared their stories with me over the past decade and all those First Nations people who have taught me so much about the world I could never have known or understood without them.

— Sylvia Olsen

Thomas

1

SUMMER HOLIDAYS WERE THE BEST. THOMAS GOT UP EARLY every morning and, after doing a few chores for his mom like shaking the rugs and hauling water from the well, headed down to the beach. Then he, Eric and Leonard spent the days climbing and swimming. Sometimes they built elaborate sand villages with logs, kelp, rocks and sand. Other times they dug up an arrowhead or grinding stone. They imagined their grandfathers and great-grandfathers hunting ducks and geese or maybe chasing away the Northern People with bows and arrows.

Summer days were endless. In the evening the boys played Monopoly at Thomas' house until long after dark, when his mom chased Leonard and Eric home.

But the best thing was fishing with Dad. Five o'clock, sometimes as early as four-thirty, was time to get up on fishing days. The sky and the trees and the hills of the Malahat Ridge blended together in muted shades of grey. The cool air nipped the end of his nose and the scent of salt water made Thomas think of hauling in salmon—a big pink, a chum or maybe even a coho.

Fishing was never as good as it was during the summer of 1955, just before Thomas entered grade four. Dad had been laid off at the mill and it was the first summer Thomas fished alongside him like a real fisherman.

On the morning just four days before school was to start, Dad tiptoed into Thomas' bedroom past Wilson and Joey's mattress. He reached down and tapped Thomas on the head.

"Come on, Thomas. I'm heading down to the beach to load up the canoe."

Thomas pushed Roger over and tucked the blanket back around his little brother. It took less than two minutes to pull up his pants and throw on a T-shirt. He slipped his feet into his shoes, which were waiting by the door, and ran down the path to catch up to Dad.

By the time they reached the beach, Thomas was wide awake. The morning air was chilly. He rubbed his arms to get rid of the goosebumps.

"Brrrr."

As usual, the canoe was upturned, waiting on the beach. Dad put the fishbox down and then lifted the canoe into the water and placed his tackle box near the back. Then he carefully rested the gaff, net and fishing rods under the seats. The two bent down and washed their hands in the cold, salty water. Dad smiled as he surveyed the canoe and Thomas, who was standing by, ready to go. Then he turned, faced the water and said a quiet prayer. "Great Creator, it is a good day. Let the fish be many, let our lines be busy and let our boat be full. We are thankful for the food these waters supply our people to keep them strong."

Dad stood a moment longer and looked out over the water. He watched the gulls in the distance circling over by the cement factory, then he studied the high white clouds that moved briskly across the sky toward the south. The tide was running swiftly this morning.

"It's gonna be a good day today, Thomas," Dad said. He held the canoe steady while Thomas stepped in. Once Thomas was settled, Dad got in and sat in the rear of the canoe. Soon they were paddling out into the bay.

"I can feel it in my bones. Take a deep breath, son. You can smell the fish," Dad laughed.

Thomas closed his eyes and breathed in until the cool air filled the deepest places in his lungs. Sure enough, he could detect the faint scent of smoke in the air.

He giggled.

"I can smell it, Dad. Fried. Dried. No, I think it's smoked salmon."

"That's it. I knew you were a real fisherman."

The water was as smooth as ice. The only sound in the bay was a quiet *plip, plip* of the fishing lines as they hit the water.

"Right here, son. They're going to be biting here today," Dad said with authority as he studied the tides and the seagulls circling over the bay.

They anchored their rods between their feet and knees and continued to gently paddle the canoe around an invisible oval.

It wasn't long before Dad started telling his fish stories.

"When I was a boy there were so many fish in this bay, you could walk on their backs from Tsartlip all the way clear across to Malahat. If the winds didn't catch up on you. That's right, son. There were so many fish in this bay, they were like a bridge clear over to the other side.

"And you know what else," Dad continued. "When your grandfather took me fishing, when I was small like you, we made sure we didn't stop paddling or the salmon would jump right in. Sometimes there were enough salmon to swamp the canoe."

The fish weren't jumping in the canoe that morning, but they were jumping in front of the canoe and on both sides. As Dad reeled one salmon in, Thomas' line bent with the weight of another tugging fish. Thomas checked the small fish carefully to make sure they measured as long as the marks Dad had carved into the side of the canoe. If a fish was too small, Thomas would have to be gentle when he released it back into the water. If the scales were harmed, the salmon would not live to grow to a good size.

They had five fish each before the sun burned through the grey sky. The water was choppy now as they pulled in the lines. Waves lapped into the canoe, which was sitting low in the water from the weight of the salmon.

"The fish have given us enough this morning," said Dad. "The Creator always makes sure our people have enough. Not too much and not too little. You take too much and the fish won't come back to us next year. You take too little and the people starve. The Creator works it out."

Back on shore, they placed the fish one on top of the other in the fishbox they'd left on the beach. Thomas bent down to lift up one side of the full box. Dad carefully packed the gaff, net and rods under his arm and lifted the other end.

"Wait until your mother sees our catch today. That'll make her smile, eh! You can take one to your grandparents and one for Uncle Joe too. And we need to deliver one to Eva and Ernie. It's hard for them to get around these days. Maybe we'll go see them together, see if they need any help with anything."

They arrived back home before Mom had even started making breakfast.

"Well, son," Dad said after they slid the fish into the wash basin behind the house, "another summer of fishing is over for you. Back to school next week—is that what your mother said? It's hard to believe the summer is over already." Dad would have kept the boys home for the fall fishing season, if he had his way, but Mom was determined to send them to school.

Thomas nodded as Dad handed him a knife. He slit open a giant chum and carefully pulled out the sac of glistening pink eggs, packed tightly together in rows. Thomas' little fingers meticulously scooped the blood out and rinsed the fish clean.

Dad watched his son proudly and then joined in.

He took the clean fish and sliced off the head and dropped it into a bucket. They weren't finished until each fish was filleted and ready to smoke. Then they placed the bones in another bucket to be returned to the water, and the eggs, in their filmy sacs, carefully in a large enamel bowl, ready to boil.

"You're a good fisherman. You kept up to me today."

Dad paused as he watched Thomas wash the last fish and toss it back into the box.

"A man who gets up early in the morning will never be hungry. My grandfather always told me, 'A man who can fill his canoe is a rich man.'"

Thomas didn't know what he liked best about fishing with Dad, the stories and the teachings of his grandfathers, or the look on Mom's face when she saw the fish in the box.

"My, my, my." Mom came out onto the porch and peered into the fishbox. "We have a real fisherman here, Abraham. Just look at the work he has done."

Thomas felt proud inside.

Once the school year began there wouldn't be much fishing—only weekends, if Thomas was lucky. Every morning would be like every other morning. Each morning would have the same rhythm.

2

THOMAS LAY IN HIS BED WITH HIS EYES CLOSED. ROGER WAS snuggled beside him, fast asleep like a cat snoozing next to a wood stove. Roger always made sure he was as close as possible. If Thomas moved, Roger moved.

Roger and Thomas shared the mattress under the window. Thomas got the window because he was the oldest. Wilson and Joey shared the mattress next to the door. You couldn't fit one more mattress into the bedroom. There was just enough space to walk around, except where the mattresses butted up together. You *could* get around them—that is, if you stepped over the clothes and fishing gear and bike tires.

Once, Wilson tried to claim the mattress under the window. He said Thomas should trade—he and Joey should get it for a change. That's because he wanted to be first out of the house in case it ever caught fire. But if anyone was going to climb out the window first, it was going to be Thomas.

They wouldn't have even thought about a fire if it hadn't been for Dad.

"That window is your way out if there is ever a fire in this house," Dad told the boys one night as he tucked them into bed.

It turned out not to be a very good bedtime story.

"When I was a kid the wood stove got so hot one night that it burned our whole house down. Lucky for me, I got out, and so did Mom and Dad and my brothers and sisters, except for Levi. He was the youngest." Dad looked down at the floor. "He never made it.

"The morning after the fire, us kids went back to look at what was left of our house. When we got there, there was a kind of blue smoky haze that just sort of hung there in the early morning sunlight. And on the ground there was only one little square—burned black as coal. Didn't even look big enough for a house. Just a pile of ashes, a couple of metal chair frames and the old wood stove with a crumpled stove-pipe leaning against it."

After telling the story Dad looked off in the distance. The boys waited for him to tell them more about Levi, but he never did.

That's why the boys were all so particular about their sleeping arrangements.

That morning the house was warm and Thomas was comfortable. Roger was snoring in his ear. Thomas squeezed his eyes shut tight and listened to the rain falling gently on the roof. He breathed in deeply and smelled the leaves drying and the blackberries left on the bushes outside, thick like jam.

Dad had already left to go fishing and Mom quietly shuffled around the house, making sure she didn't wake up the twins. They slept in the living room with her and Dad—if you could call it a living room. The space was half blocked off from the kitchen by a doorpost and a heavy grey curtain where Mom pinned important messages, cards and things the boys did at school.

Soon Thomas heard Mom stuffing a piece of wood in the stove. *Clang, bang, scrape.* Thomas lay still, enjoying the last few minutes of comfort until the smell of fresh scough bread came drifting through the room.

Time to get up.

"Wils." Thomas sat up and leaned over Roger. "Wils, you have to get up now and get ready for school."

He looked down at Roger lying there snoring like nothing was going on.

"Wils," Thomas called louder. "Come on. We gotta get going."

Joey jumped up from behind Wilson and shouted, "If Wils gets to go to school, I wanna come too."

"No way, Joey, you have to be six before you get to come to school. And Mom and Dad said you might have to wait till you are seven like Wils."

All the kids were two years apart, right down to the twins. Thomas was nine, almost ten. Then Wilson was seven, Joey was five, Roger was three and the twins were one year old.

"Come on, Wils. You have to get up now. I can smell the bread's cooked and we can't be late," Thomas said impatiently.

Ever since Wilson started school, Thomas had to make sure he got up and got ready. Wilson always pretended to be asleep like Roger, but he couldn't fool Thomas. Wilson just didn't like going to school. In fact, Wilson didn't like doing anything much except hanging around and helping Mom. Or maybe playing marbles if the boys let him win once in a while.

"Get up, Wils!" Thomas shouted. "I know you're awake. Just get up."

"I don't wanna go to school anymore, Thomas. Joey

doesn't have to go to school."

Not this again, Thomas thought.

"I wanna stay home and play with Roger," Wilson whined. "Mom says Roger misses us when we go to school. Joey won't even play with him. Come on, Thomas," he begged. "You tell Mom I should stay home with Roger. She will listen to you."

"Wils, Dad will whip your butt if you cry about going to school again. Get up. We gotta go. And you better start looking after yourself in the morning." Thomas tried to straighten out Wilson's shirt collar and flatten out his hair, which was sticking straight up. "And why don't you brush your own hair? You look like a rooster that just lost bad in a fight."

Annoyed, Thomas left his little brother and walked into the kitchen.

"Morning, Mom," he said.

Mom was quiet. She turned away and stared out the window. She looked strange, like she had something on her mind that she didn't want to say. So Thomas just carried on.

"Morning, Mom," he repeated. "That bread sure smells good."

Mom stepped closer to the window, as if she was trying to see if the Charlies next door had made it home last night or if Ernie's cow had gotten loose again.

"Mom," he said, "if Wils doesn't smarten up he's gonna get in trouble at school. Sister Madeleine says he has to brush his hair and wash up before he gets to school."

Talking about Wilson, especially when he was in trouble, usually got Mom's attention.

Thomas continued, "Yeh, Sister Madeleine says his hands are dirty like he hasn't washed them all summer. She took him into the washroom yesterday and scrubbed his hands until he cried, and then Nelson ran around like an idiot and called Wils a baby."

"Hmmm." That was it. She just kept looking way up the hill.

Mom finally turned away from the window. Carefully she lifted the bread out of the baking pan on the stove. She placed it on a plate, then put the steaming bread on the table. She gently laid some butter down beside the bread right in front of Thomas.

He knew then there was something different about that morning. He knew it when Mom laid the butter down on the table. It was a fine thing and a special day when they got butter.

Thomas carefully spread a little butter on the hot bread, then scooped a spoonful of blackberry jam on top.

"Hurry up, Wils. Come and get some. We got butter today," Thomas called out with a mouthful of breakfast.

Mom sat down as Wilson finally came into the kitchen. She lifted him onto her lap and tore off a large piece of the bread and began to butter it for him.

"You better wash your hands better than that," Thomas said as Wilson reached for his breakfast, "and you better hurry up. I'm not going to be late because of you. Mom, tell Wils to hurry up."

"I want to go with them." Joey joined them at the table and started digging into the butter. "Mom, if Wils gets to go to school, I want to go too." He wouldn't give up. "It's no fair. I have to stay home all day with the little kids. Roger doesn't even know how to play marbles."

"Shut up, Joey," Thomas said. "Just shut up and leave some of that butter for the rest of us."

Why couldn't they just send Joey to school and let Wilson stay home? It would be a lot easier. Joey would do anything, although he never knew when to shut up.

Mom stroked Wilson's hair. Every time she gently laid it

flat, it just popped back up again. She rebuttoned his shirt so the holes matched the buttons and it wasn't all bunched up. Then she straightened out his collar again.

When Wilson finished eating his bread, Mom licked her fingers and wiped the jam off his mouth and cheeks.

"Thomas," she said. "You watch out for Wils. Don't let the boys tease him. And make sure his hands are clean so those sisters don't scrub him until he cries." Mom looked out the window again, this time way up the field.

"Hurry up, Wils," Thomas said. He picked up his books from the shelf and headed out the door. He turned to make sure Wilson was following him.

"Mom, tell Joey not to follow us. The sisters said he's too young and he's not allowed to play up there at the school." Thomas pushed Joey back in the house.

"Joey will come home, Thomas. You watch out for Wils," Mom said, coming up behind the boys. She hugged Thomas with one arm and then Wilson with the other. She held on tightly for a few seconds and then let go. She placed her hands on Wilson's shoulders and guided him toward the path.

"Go on now, Wils." She patted his hair down one last time. "Thomas will take care of you. You'll be okay."

Thomas looked back at his mom. She stood motionless with her hand suspended in the air as if she didn't want to finish waving goodbye. Something sure is strange with Mom this morning, Thomas thought. Then he grabbed Wilson by the shirt and dragged him up the path. When they started running, sure enough, Joey was trailing right behind.

"You better get home," Thomas called back. "You're gonna get in trouble—I'm telling you."

It was bad enough that he couldn't get rid of Joey, but then Nelson Charlie caught up to them halfway up the hill.

"Hey, Thomas!" he called out as he ran up behind. "Still

dragging Wimpy Willy to school with you, huh?"

That was just like Nelson. He always had to make sure he picked on the small guys.

"Lay off, Nelson," Thomas said.

"Want to play marbles with me later, Wils? I got two red ones to stick in your ears." Nelson started dancing around and poking at Wilson like a tough guy. "What do you say, Wils? What do you say?"

By this time Wilson was whimpering and hanging on to Thomas' shirt.

"Get lost, Nelson. Pick on someone your own size," Thomas said, and he and Wilson hurried to the top of the hill just in time to hear the first assembly bell ring.

3

WHEN THOMAS AND WILSON ROUNDED THE CORNER OF THE school, a group of kids were crowded around the front of the school, leaning on two big, black cars. The cars were so shiny they looked like someone had spit on a cloth and shone them all day. The chrome bumpers were clear as mirrors, reflecting a distorted image of Thomas as he approached. Just as he leaned forward to look in the front window, Sister Madeleine came striding toward him, swinging her yardstick.

"Don't touch those cars!" she screamed. Her voice sounded like a cat with its tail caught in the door. "If you kids touch those cars, you will get this stick right across the back of your dirty little knuckles."

Thomas had only enough time to drag his finger across the car door, picking up a few raindrops glistening on the blackness. He licked his finger and the water was warm.

The kids in the village didn't get to see cars up close much.

Tsartlip only had one street at the top of the hill that went along in front of the school and then all the way to Victoria. If you headed the other way up the road, you could get to Pauquachin village. But no one travelled much unless they could hitch a ride with someone, and hardly anyone owned a car.

Most people used a path to get around the village. They either walked or rode a bike to school or to visit family and friends. And it wasn't far to walk to the stores or the doctor's office in Brentwood where the white people lived.

The Sams were the only Tsartlip family with a vehicle. They lived up the hill on the street close to the school. They always parked their old green truck right out in front of their house. Donnie Sam was really proud of that truck.

"My parents are the richest people in this village," he told everyone. "That's why we got a truck."

Thomas dreamed of getting a car of his own. Not an old rusty truck like the Sams'. He dreamed of getting a big, shiny, new, black car like the ones that were parked in front of the school. Even the rain on the car door was warm and sweet.

By the time Thomas got into the school behind Sister Madeleine and the other kids, Wilson was already inside waiting for him. Thomas turned around and leaned back out the door.

"Joey, you better get home. Right now," he called out to his little brother, who was hanging on the gate at the edge of the schoolyard.

Inside, some of the kids were sitting on chairs and the others were standing around, talking and waiting for Sister Theresa to call the assembly to order.

Both she and Sister Madeleine were leaning against the wall, talking to two men with black hats. Thomas watched them. One man was pointing and nodding with Sister Theresa like they were discussing a plan. He pointed his finger at Nelson, and then Sister Theresa nodded her head. Then he pointed at Wilson. Sister Theresa frowned at him and then nodded her head over towards Thomas.

One of the men looked familiar. He had visited the school a few times before. His blotchy white skin was covered with freckles, and he stood a head taller than everyone. Even Sister Theresa looked small beside him.

Once the nodding and pointing stopped, Sister Theresa called out.

"Children," she said in an official voice, "I want you to be quiet now. We have two special visitors in our school this morning. Agent Macdonald, he works for the government of Canada. He is in charge of looking after Indians. And Mr. Lawson is from the Catholic Church. I would like you all to welcome them to our Tsartlip Day School this morning."

All the students clapped.

Thomas had never seen Agent Macdonald look after any-one. But today he was sure looking the Indian kids up and down, and Thomas didn't like how it made him feel. Even Sister Theresa didn't look pleased, especially when the agent pointed at Wilson and him.

The other man in the hat didn't seem interested at all. He just stood over in the corner of the hall and talked to Sister Madeleine.

"Now," Sister Theresa continued, "everyone must go to their regular class except for Nelson, Dusty, Howard, Monica, Thomas and Wilson. Agent Macdonald would like to speak to them."

Sister Theresa's thin mouth was pinched tight as she spoke, so a white line surrounded her pale, pinkish-blue lips.

All the other kids slowly filed out of the room. The chosen six huddled together. Thomas could feel Wilson tugging on his shirt.

Thomas remembered the last time the agent visited the school. That time they called out Bernice's and Charlie's names and they had to wait behind. Thomas had filed out with the rest of the kids. It was the last time anyone saw Charlie and Bernice.

Agent Macdonald waited until the last student exited the assembly room, then he began. "You have all been chosen today to go to residential school. Mr. Lawson and I are going to take you children for a long ride in those black cars."

Residential school. That meant going away—and staying away—probably for a long time. Thomas wanted to be excited at the chance of getting a car ride, but all he could feel was the pounding of his heart, thudding in his chest.

"You are going to live at the Kuper Island Residential

School for Indian children." Agent Macdonald said it as if it was something special.

All Thomas had ever heard about Kuper Island Residential School for Indians was that Dad said it would be over his dead body if any of his children went there.

"Thomas." Wilson tugged hard on Thomas' shirt. "Thomas, I don't want to go to that school." He began to sniffle. "Come on, tell them, Thomas."

Thomas looked at Sister Theresa. Then he looked at Agent Macdonald. There didn't seem to be any point in telling either of them that. Wilson's sniffles grew louder. "Tell them, Thomas, tell them."

Instead, Thomas asked, as loudly as he could, "When do we get to come home?"

"Some of you will be allowed to return to Tsartlip to see your family for the Christmas holidays. Then you will return to the school until next summer."

"How long is Christmas?" Wilson whispered. "Thomas, ask him how long is Christmas?"

"Shut up, Wils." Thomas knew Christmas was a long time away, and Wilson didn't need to hear that.

Who gets to come home at Christmas? Thomas thought. And what if we don't get to come home at Christmas? What am I going to do with Wils until Christmas or maybe even next summer?

"My grandfather said that none of the Sams were going to go to residential school. Not ever," Monica piped up. She was Donnie Sam's older sister. Their father was the Chief and their grandfather was the Chief before that.

"Don't talk back to the agent, Monica. He has already made the arrangements with your families. You children are lucky to be chosen today." Sister Theresa didn't look like she believed what she was saying.

"My father is the Chief and he'll be mad if you take me to that school. You can't just take me away without his permission. He never said anything about this to me before I left the house this morning. And what about my clothes? I have to go home to get my clothes!" Monica's knees trembled and her voice grew louder and louder. Tears began to well up in her eyes.

"The school will have all the clothes you need. And I have taken care of your father's concerns. Now I hope that will be all." Agent Macdonald was losing patience. He was in a hurry to get going.

"I don't wanna go." Wilson was crying hard now and rubbing his nose all over the back of Thomas' shirt. "Thomas, I don't wanna go away to school. I wanna go home."

Sister Theresa bent down in front of Wilson. Her forehead crinkled, forcing her eyebrows into a V shape.

"Wilson, Thomas and you have been chosen to go to the residential school. Now don't cause a fuss for these men. They have come a long way to pick you up and they are going to take good care of you."

Thomas didn't know what to think about going to the residential school. Wilson was crying and snivelling, Monica was arguing with Agent Macdonald, and the other kids, even Nelson, looked pretty worried. All Thomas wanted to think about was riding in one of those black cars. He wondered what it would be like to sit in the back and look out the windows from inside.

He wondered if the school and Sister Theresa would look different through the window. Maybe the school would look shiny and new, and maybe the sister would be smiling.

Sister Theresa led the kids outside. Agent Macdonald and the other man followed close behind, making sure, it seemed, that none of them took off and ran home.

4

WHEN THEY GOT CLOSE TO THE CARS, WORRY BEGAN TO CUT into Thomas' excitement. Dad had said his kids were never going to Kuper. Did Dad even *know* they were taking them away? And what about Mom? Maybe she'd acted so strange that morning because she'd heard what was going on.

Thomas' mind darted back to a conversation he had overheard Mom and Dad having late one night not long ago. Mom had said there was nothing they could do if the agent wanted to take the boys to residential school. "The agents are taking kids from all the villages," she said. "And if the parents try to stop them the police will throw the parents in jail."

That's when Thomas had heard Dad say it would be over his dead body that his kids would go to residential school. Jail or no jail.

Thomas frowned in confusion. Mom was afraid. That was it. Now what would Mom and Dad do if the boys didn't come home after school? What about Roger? Who would sleep with Roger? He couldn't sleep with Mom and Dad. And the twins and Joey wouldn't be any good to him.

The second he thought of Joey, Thomas saw his younger brother run around behind the cars, just as Agent Macdonald opened the door.

"You three boys will ride in my car," he said, pushing Howard into the back seat with Wilson and Thomas. Monica, Dusty and Nelson were led to the other car.

Thomas bounced as he hit the seat, then slid across to the far window. Wilson reluctantly crawled in behind him. The seats were shiny and black, just like the rest of the car. Inside it smelled like the new pair of shoes that Dad had bought a few years ago. Thomas closed his eyes and took a deep breath. He remembered the day Dad brought the shoes home.

Dad had got some steady work down in Victoria at the lumber mill. So the day before Christmas he arrived home with three huge brown bags.

"Merry Christmas," he called out as he came in the door. He put two bags in the corner then threw the other up onto the kitchen table.

"Two for you and one for me," he said as all the kids tried to look inside. "And don't be nosey Jones."

He reached into the bag and pulled out a brand-new pair of black leather shoes.

"A man like Abraham Jones should have one new pair of leather shoes in his life," he said with a smile that reached clear across his face. He bent down, slipped his feet into the shoes and carefully tied the laces.

"Now, Priscilla Jones," he said as he held his hands out to her. "Will you dance with the man with the new shoes?"

Mom gave her What's-next-Abraham look over her shoulder as they began waltzing gracefully across the room. The kitchen smelled like those new shoes for weeks after Christmas.

The memory of the shoes faded when Thomas opened his eyes. Wilson was bawling his eyes out, sitting so close he was almost right on Thomas' lap. And by this time Howard was getting upset, too, and annoyed with Wilson.

"Gawd, Wils, it's not gonna do any good to cry," he said. "Thomas, can't you shut him up?"

Agent Macdonald finally shut the car doors and climbed into the front behind the steering wheel. He turned the key and revved the gas. The car started, and Thomas could feel the soft purr of the engine underneath his legs. Just as they began to pull away, Thomas looked through the side window. Joey grabbed the door handle and began swinging back and forth. Agent Macdonald saw him through his rear-view mirror and stopped the car and opened his window.

"Get that kid off the side of the car!" he shouted to Sister Theresa.

She ran over and yanked Joey away. Once again the car began to pull away from the school. But before they got more than a car length away, Joey was hanging on to the door handle again. This time Agent Macdonald hit the brakes so hard, the boys bumped into each other in the back seat. Thomas straightened himself out and looked back out the window just as Joey bounced onto the ground.

The third time Agent Macdonald tried to take off, Joey was once again swinging from the car door, shouting into the window, "If you get to go for a car ride, Thomas, I wanna come too. It's not fair. Wils gets to go with you. Let me in."

Now Agent Macdonald was really mad. He stopped the car, leaned his head out the window and said very deliberately to Sister Theresa, "Get that boy and put him in the front seat beside me. If he wants to go to school that bad, I will take him."

"Oh, I am so sorry, Agent Macdonald. I will take care of him," she replied. "He is only five. He is far too young to go to residential school. He isn't even old enough for the Day School. I apologize—I know you are in a hurry. Here—let me, I will send him home right away."

"He will be six soon enough. He wants to go to school, Sister Theresa, so put him in. I can't be fooling around with some five-year-old all day. We have a ferry to catch." Agent Macdonald wasn't asking—he was telling. It didn't matter to him how old Joey was.

Reluctantly Sister Theresa opened the car door, and Joey jumped in the front seat beside Agent Macdonald. Before the door was completely closed, the agent hit the gas and the car sped up the road, past the Sams' green truck parked in front of their house, and down toward the ferry at the beach.

Wilson kept yanking Thomas' shirt and crying uncontrollably while Thomas tried to watch outside. It was hard, though, because the back seat was so low he couldn't see out the window without stretching his neck. Soon they were parked behind the other black car, waiting for the ferry.

Agent Macdonald turned the engine off and craned his neck around to the back seat. "This ferry will take us over to Malahat. Then we will have a long car ride to Chemainus. Once we get there, I will load you on the Kuper Island boat, and it will take you over to the school. For now, you kids stay in the car." Then the agent got out and locked the doors.

"And don't touch anything," he added before he sauntered towards the other car.

Thomas stretched up and peered out the window just in time to see Dad walk out from behind the maple trees and head toward Agent Macdonald.

Their voices were muffled through the closed windows, but Thomas could tell Dad was mad. He could hear his dad begin to shout.

"I told those nuns up at the Day School that they could teach my kids. But no kid of mine is ever going to go to that Kuper Island Residential School! What do you think you're doing, coming and taking them away like this? No one asked me if you could take my children!"

Dad turned, and for a moment, it looked like he was walking away. Then he turned back again and charged, right toward Agent Macdonald. But the other man saw Dad coming. He reached out and grabbed Dad's arms, twisting them behind his back. Dad tried to break free from the other man's grip, but Agent Macdonald pinned him against the tree.

"You can't do this!" Dad panted. "You can't take my kids! I get home from fishing this morning and Priscilla finally tells me what's going on. Said she heard what you were up to yesterday from Father Salmo, down at the church. She told me that there's nothing I can do about it. But she's got that wrong! She might be afraid of you, but I'm not!"

Again, Dad tried to break free, but Agent Macdonald and the other man kept him pinned. After a minute Dad stopped struggling and the two men loosened their grip. Then, just as Agent Macdonald was going to say something, Joey began to jump up and down in the front seat of the car.

"Look, Dad!" he called out. "I get to ride in a brand-new car. And I know how to open the window." Joey had been pulling and pushing on the window lever until he finally got the window down. Then he popped his head out, pleased with his accomplishment.

"What are you doing with Joey?" Dad completely lost control. He took a swing at Agent Macdonald and barely missed his jaw. "He just turned five! He isn't even old enough to go to the Day School. Priscilla never said anything about Joey. You can't take him!"

Dad tried to take another swing, but both men held him against the tree.

Dad had never looked so mad. But Thomas knew there wasn't one thing his dad could do about the whole mess. Thomas wanted to look away. He didn't have to watch his dad's humiliation, but he kept staring at the scene in disbelief.

"Joey!" Dad called out sternly, ignoring the men. "Joey, you get out of that car right now."

"Abraham." Agent Macdonald's white face was covered with red blotches. His hat had fallen off his head and lay rumpled on the road. His pale yellow hair stuck to the sides of his head while clumps poked straight up on top. He shook his body and straightened out his coat and pants.

"Abraham, you and I both know that the law requires all

Indian children to attend school. It has been decided that Thomas and Wilson will attend the Kuper Island Residential School. And if you stand in my way, I will see to it that you and your wife are put in jail. You know the penalty for obstructing me, Abraham. I wouldn't suggest you try it. If you contact us and make the arrangements, your children can be returned to you for ten days at Christmas. Otherwise you will see them next summer. And as for Joey, it's either now or later. He wanted to come so we brought him along. Tell Priscilla he wants to go to school with his brothers."

Thomas didn't want to see his dad back away from Agent Macdonald. Dad was always in control. Dad was always neat and tidy. But Thomas watched his dad wipe the sleeves of his shirt with firm, deliberate strokes, like they had something stuck to them. His face was pale and drawn, and his thick, dark hair stuck out at the sides and on top. He put his head down and turned away.

Dad didn't come past the car to say goodbye. He didn't even look at his boys. He looked really sad, different than he'd looked on the day that he and Mom had returned from Granny's funeral, but kind of the same, too. Slowly, Dad walked back up the hill. Thomas looked away. He tried to hold Wilson down, to block his view, but his brother kneeled and stared out the window, watching Dad retreat. Then Wilson turned around and flopped down on the seat. He hid his face behind Thomas' back and sobbed quietly.

But Joey was still excited and wouldn't shut up or sit still. He jumped up and down on the front seat and shouted, "Did you see that, Thomas? They were beating up Dad. They're gonna get in big trouble for beating up Dad, aren't they, Thomas."

When Agent Macdonald returned to the car he muttered under his breath, "They don't know what's good for them. They don't know how to be thankful. All they ever do is complain."

Thomas couldn't think of one thing they could be thankful for. Not right then. But he couldn't see what good complaining would do either, so he kept quiet.

He held on to Wilson and rubbed his younger brother's head.

"Wils, I'll figure out something to do. Really I will. It'll be okay. I promise," he whispered.

Wilson laid his head on Thomas' lap and finally went to sleep. Thomas must have slept, too, because the next thing he knew the ferry ride was over and he had missed the whole trip up to Chemainus. The car pulled into a bumpy parking lot overlooking a wharf and stopped.

Agent Macdonald jumped out and opened the car doors.

"This is the Chemainus boat dock," he said. "Time to get out and head down to the school boat."

Thomas pushed Wilson out the door and stretched his stiff legs. He slid out, then turned to look back at the car. It didn't seem as big as when it was parked in front of the Day School. It didn't glisten quite as much, now that the raindrops had dried. And when Thomas really thought about it, he realized things didn't look that good from the inside. In fact, everything looked pretty bad, especially Dad dragging his feet up the hill, leaving his boys locked inside the car. Thomas hadn't bothered to look out the windows much after that.

They staggered down the long ramp to the dock where Monica, Dusty and Nelson were already waiting. The church man had gone, leaving them alone on the wharf. Dusty and Monica huddled close to each other next to an old salmon trawler with black lettering on the side: *Monfort*.

Nelson was down at the end of the dock, checking over the boats and gear like he owned the place.

Joey ran ahead and started climbing up onto the boat.

"Come on, Joey. You stick with us." Dusty pulled him off

and tried to hold him still. Wilson followed right behind Thomas as they joined the girls, hanging on like a cat with its claws stuck in a tree.

"So what's wrong, Wils? Does the baby want his mommy?" Nelson swaggered up the dock toward them.

"Stop it, Nelson," Dusty snapped at him. "Just stop it. It's not like any of us want to be here."

The two girls put their arms around Wilson. "It's okay, Wils. We won't let Nelson bug you. We're gonna all be together."

Yeh, she's right, Thomas thought. Whatever was going to happen over at the school, at least the kids from Tsartlip could all stick together. Maybe it would be like home . . . except for Mom and Dad and Roger and the twins.

He turned and stared back at the beach. He could see the clams squirting and the water gently lapping over their tiny mounds. Thomas breathed in the familiar salty sea air and listened closely for the *shlt, shlt,* but he couldn't hear the clams. The loud din of a giant pulp mill drowned them out.

Agent Macdonald locked the car doors and followed the kids. When he arrived at the boat, he greeted an old man who emerged from the cabin.

"Afternoon, Jim," Agent Macdonald said and shook the man's hand. "We've got a load for you—seven here from Tsartlip. Think you can fit them all into this boat of yours?"

"No problem at all, Agent. There's room for you, too."

"No, thanks. You can count me out," Agent Macdonald laughed. "They're all yours. I'm finished with them. They're expecting six of them over at Kuper, but tell Father Maynard that I brought an extra one along, will you? I couldn't get rid of the youngest Jones boy—the little one over there. So I brought him along for good measure."

The two men talked for a few minutes. Then Agent

Macdonald gave Jim a paper. "That's Nelson, Monica and Dusty and Howard," he said, referring to the note. Then he added quietly, "And you can tell Father Maynard to be ready for some trouble from the Jones boys. The middle one won't stop crying and the youngest is nothing but a handful."

When he was finished, Agent Macdonald turned towards the kids. "Okay, kids, this is the end of the road for me. I've got things to do so I am going to leave you here with Jim. He'll take you across to Kuper Island. Don't worry about a thing. You're in good hands."

Agent Macdonald looked happy to be leaving and Thomas was happy to see him go. Thomas looked closely at the boatman. He looked like he could be someone's grandfather. His thick, white hair poked out from under his cap and the lines around his clear blue eyes made him look like he was permanently smiling.

"Jump in," Jim said in a cheery voice. "You will all have to crowd together. There are only two benches in the cabin for you kids to sit on. The rest of the boat is full of supplies for the school. It's going to take us about an hour, so make yourselves as comfortable as you can."

Monica and Dusty piled in first and tucked Joey in between them. Nelson shared the bench with them while Howard, Thomas and Wilson faced them on the other side. Jim fired up the engine and soon they took off. Almost immediately, Thomas felt a sharp pang. He bent over, gripping his stomach. It was then he realized he hadn't eaten since the scough bread with butter and jam at breakfast. It seemed like a year ago and he was starving.

"My stomach is screaming hungry," he said to the rest of them.

A few nodded and mumbled a reply. "Yeh, no kidding, so am I."

Wilson pulled Thomas' head down and whispered in his ear. "I'm not hungry, Thomas. I don't want to eat. Not until Mom feeds us."

"You better eat something before that, Wils," Thomas replied, then turned to the others. "I wonder when we'll get something to eat. Do you think they'll feed us supper once we get over there?"

"They better," Nelson said, "'cause if they don't, I'll have to go and find some food myself. My stomach is sucking in. It's really sucking in, man, I don't know if I'm gonna make it."

Joey was finally sitting still. "I hope you can get me something to eat too, Nelson. I'm really hungry and I don't feel so good."

Thomas' head was light and he closed his eyes. Time passed. It seemed like hours later when Jim stuck his head in the cabin door and said, "Heads up, kids." He pointed out the window. "Take a look at your new school. Kuper Island Residential School."

Jim cut the motor and the boat bumped up against the wharf. He jumped out, hauled the thick ropes off the deck and began looping them around the posts.

Thomas pulled himself up onto his knees and peered out the window. The boat was tied up at the end of a long, narrow, red wharf. His eyes followed the red handrail to the end of the wharf where a little lane wound its way around the beach and up into the trees. Across the lane a path led up a hill and between two gigantic trees to a huge building perched right on top.

Thomas' mouth fell open in awe. It must be Kuper Island Residential School, but it was more than he had ever imagined. This was not just a school—it was the most impressive building Thomas had ever seen. The sun glistened from the long rows of windows stacked one on top of the other. The red bricks and large wooden doors looked beautiful and ominous at the same time.

"Wow," Thomas said quietly.

"Wow. Wow," he heard the other kids repeat one after the other as they looked up at the school looming over them.

Nelson didn't say a word. He kept his head down and didn't even look out the window.

One by one Jim helped the kids climb out of the boat. Thomas' legs wobbled as he made his way towards the school. The group was so tightly stuck together that they tripped over each other's feet.

"Don't take all day. They're waiting for you," Jim said, coming up behind them.

As they neared the school building, Thomas saw four men and two women waiting on the front stairs. They were dressed in black Catholic gowns.

When they reached the stairs, Jim stepped in front of the kids, who were still huddled together. He reached over and shook the hand of the man who stood in the middle of the group. The man was almost as wide as he was tall and his long black gown heaved up and down as well as in and out each time he took a breath.

"Good afternoon, Father Maynard. I have brought seven from Tsartlip for you. I think they are all from the Day School. Agent Macdonald said the little one is an extra. Apparently, he didn't want to stay home."

Almost on cue, Joey began to cry. Thomas put his arm around his little brother and whispered, "Don't worry, Joey, it'll be okay." He wished he could believe his own words.

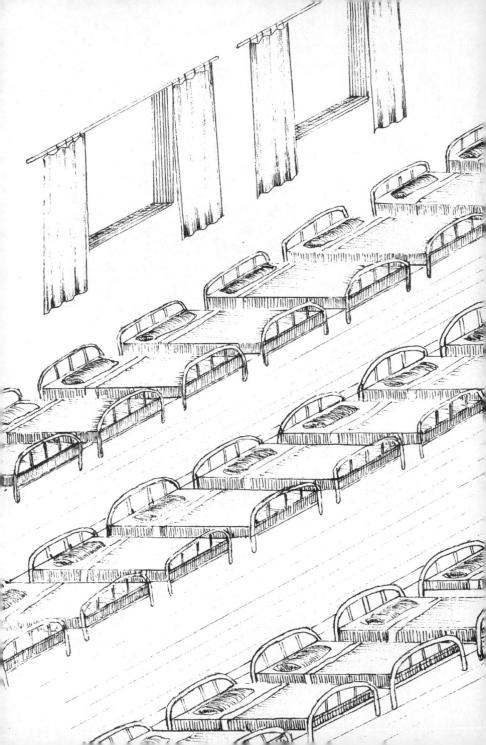

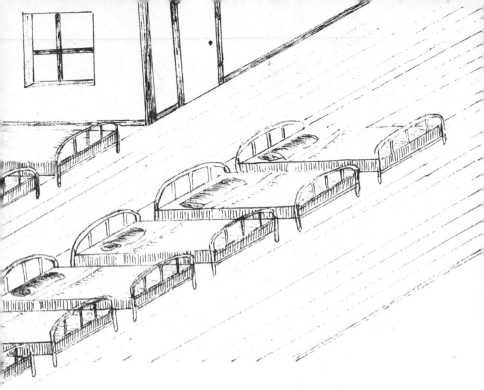

Wilson

1

WILSON THOUGHT ABOUT THAT DAY IN THE SUMMER. HE
AND JOEY were playing with Elmer and Alex Charlie. They
were digging clams after supper when suddenly the George
family, who were cooking dinner just down the beach, all
started shouting and jumping around.

The four boys ran down the beach. As they arrived, Sam
and Ned George dove into the water and started swimming
like crazy.

In the bay a canoe was heading right for the beach. Sitting

in the canoe was old man Edward, flapping his hands.

"Dad! Dad!" Sam and Ned shouted as they swam out. "We're coming. Just hold on!"

The sons pulled the canoe to shore, grabbed their dad and dragged him onto the beach. By then old Edward was as blue as a jaybird and his eyes were rolled back so far, only the whites showed.

Everyone was rushing around telling each other what to do.

"Sit him up!" someone shouted. "No, lay him down!"

No one knew what to do. There he was, lying on the beach, dying right before their eyes. Then Joey grabbed onto Wilson's hand and squeezed it tight. Wilson squeezed back. He was feeling pretty scared himself, especially when Mary George started crying that her old man was going to die. It wasn't until Ned and Sam pushed hard on their dad's chest that a peanut popped out of his mouth like a cork and he started breathing again.

That day seemed like a long time ago and far away.

Now Wilson stood in front of the biggest building he had ever seen. He stretched his neck right back till it hurt, and he still couldn't take in the whole scene.

Everyone looked scared. Even Nelson—his head was down as he shifted uneasily from one foot to the other.

The nuns and priests stood in a line, eyeing the group of kids all huddled together.

Jim rummaged around in his pocket. "Now let me see," he said as he pulled out the paper Agent Macdonald had given him. "I have my introductions written down here somewhere."

He turned towards the girls and tapped Monica on the head. "This is Monica, so this young woman over here must be Dusty," he said.

After he introduced Nelson and Howard, he finally said,

"And these are the Joneses. Thomas is the oldest and this one is Wilson." He reached around to touch Wilson's shoulder. "Agent Macdonald said this little boy wasn't very happy about coming to school. He cried and hollered until he fell asleep in the car."

Wilson shrank away from the man's hand and tucked his head behind Thomas, now looking ashamed as well as frightened.

Thomas turned around, kicked Wilson in the ankle and scowled. "Now look what you did," he whispered angrily under his breath.

"And then this one here is Joey Jones." Jim reached over and mussed Joey's hair. "He's only five, but the agent had a little trouble with him as well. He wanted to come too, I guess, so Agent Macdonald brought him along," Jim added, laughing. "Said he'd send one more for good measure."

"Now, kids," Jim said, "let me introduce you to Father Maynard. He is the principal of your new school."

Jim pointed to the short, fat man standing in the middle of the group. Beads of sweat ran down the man's forehead. He had a small dimple where a chin would normally be and three chins, hanging one on top of the other, over his tight, white church collar.

"And this is Brother Eubieus, Brother Jerry and Brother Henry Philipe." Jim pointed at the younger men standing beside the fat man. "They are the teachers for the boys. Sister Dominique and Sister Mary Louise are the girls' teachers."

Sister Mary Louise stood on the other side of Father Maynard and was just about the same size. She had long, black hairs on her chin and under her nose. It looked to Wilson like she was staring at him, but he couldn't tell for sure. Her eyes looked like black glass beads behind her thick, dark-rimmed glasses. Her forehead wrinkled in a scowl, forcing her bushy, black eyebrows together.

As soon as Jim finished the introductions, he said good-bye and turned toward his boat. Wilson's chest began to tighten under his shirt. He gasped for breath. It felt like a rubber band was being pulled tighter and tighter around his windpipe. He wanted to run and follow Jim, but he rubbed his hands against his chest instead, hoping to relieve the pressure.

Don't leave us here, Wilson thought as he watched Jim saunter down the wharf. Please come back and take us with you.

A lump formed in his throat and he couldn't swallow it. "Don't cry, Wils," he whispered to himself. "Don't cry, Wils. Thomas will be really mad if you cry. Just don't cry this time."

Wilson glanced over at Nelson. He hoped the older boy wasn't looking. Nelson would only make matters worse. He'd start jumping and pointing and calling Wilson "Wimpy Willy" or "Illy Willy" or "Frills," like he always did. Wilson surprised himself when he sucked in hard and held back his tears.

"Now," Father Maynard said in a loud voice, "we want to welcome you all to Kuper Island Residential School for Indian children. The nuns and brothers will take you to the dormitories where you will sleep, and they will show you around the school. You must listen to them very closely so you won't get lost."

Wilson looked at all the windows lined up and stacked on top of each other. He checked to see whether any windows were open, but he couldn't tell. What would it be like inside the building? He imagined running from one window to another, trying to find a way out. He held a long breath as he tried to figure out how he would find the door.

"Dusty and Monica will go with Sister Mary Louise to the senior girls' dorm." As soon as the priest spoke, Monica let go of Joey's hand and followed Dusty and the nun into the front door of the school.

"Howard and Nelson will go with Brother Jerry."

Nelson didn't appear to be paying attention. He kicked a stone from one foot to the other.

"Nelson?" Father Maynard looked around.

Nelson stopped when he heard his name the second time. He lifted his head as Brother Jerry walked toward him. Nelson stood straight up and puffed out his chest. Wilson drew in a deep breath and held it.

"Yeh, I'm Nelson," he said, looking the brother right in the eye. "Did he say you were gonna show me around? What did he say your name was? Brother Fairy?"

The brother wasn't much bigger than Nelson. He had a skinny face and bony, white hands with long fingernails. He didn't look very tough, but Wilson could tell from the squint in his eye that he was mean.

"He said you are coming with me. He said my name is Brother Jerry. And I'm saying right now . . . Nelson, is that your name—Nelson? I'm saying right now, mister smart mouth, that you better watch what you say to me."

Wilson tucked himself against Thomas and held onto Joey. There was a moment of silence as Nelson and the brother eyeballed each other. Then, without a word, they took off into the school with Howard following behind.

Wilson opened his mouth. "Phew," he said as he slowly released his breath. He had never heard anyone talk to Nelson like that.

Sister Dominique, Brother Henry Philipe, Brother Eubieus and Father Maynard were now facing Thomas, Wilson and Joey. Wilson pressed hard against his brothers, safely out of the piercing view of nuns and priests.

"So, what do we have left?" Father Maynard said, looking

the boys up and down. "It looks to me like we have the Jones family."

He stepped toward Thomas and smiled. His enormous cheeks, which hung loosely in folds beside his full mouth, gathered and lifted in dimples that almost hid his eyes. Wilson couldn't tell if it was a real smile or if the sun was too bright.

Father Maynard came closer. "It *is* Thomas, isn't it? Thomas Jones."

He held the list of names up and smiled again, this time at the paper. "Thomas Jones—you are nine years old, almost ten it appears. You will go with Brother Henry Philipe."

Thomas turned and tried to loosen his younger brothers' grips.

No, Wilson thought. No. This can't be happening. He hadn't thought about it before. Not Thomas. Thomas had to look after him. Mom said.

"I have to go with Brother Henry Philipe," Thomas said. "You guys have to let go of me." Joey was holding on as tightly as Wilson by now.

"No. No. What about me?" Wilson sputtered. "What about me? Thomas, you can't go without me."

Thomas put one arm around Wilson and pulled Joey close with the other. He hugged them tightly.

"We have to go with Thomas," Joey blurted, pulling away. "Thomas takes care of us. Mom and Dad say that's how it goes with us."

Deep folds formed across Father Maynard's forehead as he glared down at them.

"Well, little boy," he said, "that's not how it goes around here. At this school you will go where you are told, and Thomas will go where he is told. And you aren't old enough to go with your brother."

Wilson grabbed onto Thomas' belt. "Thomas. Tell them. Tell them you have to look after me. Tell them the Joneses stick together. Like Dad says. And Mom told you to look after me. Before we went to school this morning, remember? She told you to watch out for me." He squeezed his eyes tight.

Finally Thomas spoke up. "I can't go without my brothers. Mom told me to take care of Wils, and Joey isn't even supposed to be here. Dad said he is too young. Joey has to go home."

Father Maynard shrugged. "That's very nice that you want to take care of your brothers, young man. But your Dad isn't here and you are going with Brother Henry Philipe to the dorm."

2

THOMAS FOLLOWED THE BROTHER INTO THE SCHOOL. JOEY held on tight to Wilson's hand. The two little boys waited in silence.

"These are the two we are going to have trouble with, I suppose," Father Maynard said sharply. "Well, Brother Eubieus, I hope you will show them how we expect them to behave here at Kuper."

The tall man who moved toward them had fluffy, yellow hair hanging over his ears and across his forehead. His bright blue eyes twinkled as he flashed a broad smile from ear to ear. Brother Eubieus reached out his large hands and almost scooped the small boys up.

Wilson and Joey each took a hand and entered the giant doors at the front of the school. Inside, a huge staircase twisted up to the ceiling. The high, heavy wooden railings glistened in the late-afternoon sun. Brother Eubieus led the way up the stairs. Wilson paused as he examined the darkly polished wood under his feet. In the railing he could see a distorted reflection of his face bobbing up and down with each stair he climbed. It didn't really look like him except for his hair, which stuck straight up on top.

"We are going up to the third floor," Brother Eubieus said. "That's where you boys will sleep. I am going to find you both a bed, some school clothes and a locker so you can put your things away."

When the stairs finally stopped, Brother Eubieus led the boys through a high door frame and down a long wide corridor. It was empty. There was no furniture, no chairs or tables—only dark wood-panelled walls and heavy planked floors that shone like glass. Placed evenly between the large doors hung pictures of old kings and queens like the ones at the Day School. Sister Theresa always told stories about them although Wilson couldn't remember what the stories were about. He studied the polished brass doorknobs and keyholes as they passed the closed doors. The doorknobs were too big for his hands.

They walked all the way to the end of the corridor, then Brother Eubieus stopped and opened a door.

"This is your dorm," he said. He bent down on one knee and patted the boys' shoulders. "I know you boys are scared. This must be very different from your house. But if we stick together it'll be all right. I am here to look after you, so how about we try to make the best of it."

Wilson looked around the room. One whole wall was windows. Thick, red curtains hung neatly at the sides of the long, narrow windows, like giant guards lined up next to each other. There were ten, maybe twenty beds—too many for him to count. One row faced the windows and the other faced the wall. A narrow pathway separated the ends of the

beds. Each bed had matching pale yellow blankets tucked in tight and flat with identical folds at the foot and pillows at the head. It didn't look to him like anyone had ever slept in the room before.

Wilson thought of Mom. What would she think if she looked at all these beds? She was always trying to get Thomas and him to clean up their room and roll their blankets up in the morning. But he didn't think Mom would like this bedroom.

He thought about Mondays. Monday was washday. Mom would get up early and fill the stove to the brim with dry alder and fir logs to heat the water. When the boys were awake she'd come into their room.

"Washday," she'd say with a cheery voice. "Blankets and all."

Sometimes Wilson would lie on top of the dirty piles of laundry out on the back porch. He'd listen to the swish swoosh of the old wringer washer while he'd watch Mom hang load after load on the clothesline strung between the porch post and the large oak at the edge of the field.

Later in the afternoon Mom would return to the boys' room with armloads of freshly dried laundry. She'd tuck the clean blankets onto the mattresses and pile the neatly folded clothes in baskets stacked in the corner.

Wilson loved the room after Mom finished. It felt safe and comfortable.

Was it Monday today? The room was spotless and polished, not a thing out of place. In fact, there wasn't anything in the room at all. Not a sock, or a shirt or a pair of shorts. There were no toys, no fishing gear, no buckets or clam-shells. Nothing. Where were the kids? Where was their stuff?

Brother Eubieus sat on a bed near the door and lifted the boys up. He placed Wilson on his one side and Joey on the other.

"I am new, too. I just started working here a few weeks ago." Wilson felt protected under Brother Eubieus' arms. "You know, boys, the first time I saw this room it looked a little strange to me, too. It doesn't look like my bedroom at home."

Joey was silent. Wilson couldn't think of anything to say. Then Brother Eubieus continued, "Too tidy, don't you think? Don't worry. You will get used to it. I come from a big family. They live a long way from here. I really miss them."

Wilson wasn't afraid of Brother Eubieus. Joey didn't seem to be, either. He climbed onto the brother's lap. "When am I going to go home?" Joey asked. "I want to go home now."

"You won't be going home for a long time, Joey. How about if we stick together here? Now, let's find a bed and some new clothes. Would you like that?"

He led the boys to two beds next to the window.

"This will be your bed, Wilson. And Joey's will be right next to yours."

"We don't need two beds," Wilson muttered. "This one

will be all right for both of us."

"You don't have to share a bed with your brother. You are lucky here."

Brother Eubieus didn't understand.

"But I don't want to have my own bed," Wilson insisted.

"I don't want my own bed, either," Joey added. "I sleep with Wils. We don't sleep in beds like this."

Joey grabbed onto the blankets and swung his leg up onto the bed.

"Joey's gonna fall off. The bed's too high," Wilson said. "We sleep on mattresses on the floor."

"Joey will be okay," Brother Eubieus said soothingly. "You'll be right next to him. You can look after him."

Wilson didn't like how that sounded. *You can look after him.* How could he look after Joey? He began to worry again. He looked at Brother Eubieus. He was kind and gentle, but he didn't know. He didn't know anything about Wilson or Joey or what Mom had said about Thomas watching out for them. Wilson held on to his stomach—it felt hollow.

"What about Thomas?" Joey was bouncing on the bed. "Let's go sleep with Thomas, Wils."

Brother Eubieus lifted Joey onto the floor. "Thomas will sleep in the room right across the hall. You will sleep here next to Wilson. And soon you will have new friends, too."

Wilson didn't want to meet new friends. He didn't want his own bed. And he didn't want to look after Joey. He just wanted to go home.

Brother Eubieus took the boys over to a huge bin of clothes. Inside were heavy denim pants and rough cotton shirts made out of rice sacks. Just as they began looking through them, a loud *Clang! Clang! Clang!* rang out. Wilson jumped up and grabbed onto Joey. His heart thumped and his knees collapsed beneath him as he fell back against the bed.

Brother Eubieus laughed. "Don't be afraid of the bell, Wilson. It rings all the time. This one is the supper bell. Come on, boys, get these clothes into your cubbyholes and let's hurry downstairs. You must be starving."

"Yeah, I'm hungry!" Joey exclaimed. "Let's go eat, Wils."

Wilson felt empty, but not hungry.

They finished up with the clothes and hurried down the corridor to the stairs. Over the railing they saw a long line of girls at the bottom. Monica and Dusty stood at the end of the line. At first the girls were hard to recognize because they had short new haircuts. Joey made a beeline down the stairs and jumped straight into Monica's arms.

"Joey, come back here." Brother Eubieus hurried after him. "You can't run off like that. Listen, boys and girls are separated at Kuper. You and Wilson stay together and line up with the boys."

Together they caught up to the boys filing into the dining hall. Inside was a maze of grey painted tables and matching benches.

Wilson quickly looked around. "Where's Thomas?" he asked.

"Oh, he's probably with the older boys," Brother Eubieus said. Wilson looked around anxiously for Thomas or Howard—anyone from home. The room was a jumble of faces he didn't know. Everyone was talking at once, some shouting, others laughing. Wilson sat down and placed the palms of his hands tightly over his ears and rested his forehead on the table in front of him. His mind went black.

3

AT KUPER, WILSON'S WORLD BECAME A BLUR OF BELLS. ALL day bells rang for classes, bells rang for meals and bells rang for prayers. Kids ran here and there, talking loudly or laughing out of control. Boys pushed each other around and said swear words he knew that Dad would never put up with.

Brother Eubieus tried to teach Wilson the ropes. But soon there were so many directions that Wilson couldn't distinguish one thing from the next. "Wilson, make sure you are in the dining hall right on time." "Wilson, make sure you clean the dirt from under your nails." "Wilson, you must eat something." "Wilson, stand still and close your eyes when Father Maynard is saying prayers."

Mealtimes were the worst. Although Wilson's stomach felt empty, he didn't want to eat. Sometimes it made a loud noise and stabbed with sharp pains.

Brother Eubieus tried to encourage him. "Wilson," he'd say as he sat next to the boy, "it's not so bad."

One day the brother set a plate of soft mashed potatoes, boiled carrots and a small piece of grey meat in front of Wilson. He watched the meat swim around in a puddle of thin, watery liquid, then finally settle. The corners curled up slightly, and a wide grain of lumpy fat divided the piece almost in two. He didn't know exactly what kind of meat it was, but it didn't smell like anything he should eat.

With both hands he suspended his chin above his plate and examined the food. He gagged at the unpleasant odour. The meat had to be mouldy or something. He remembered Mom saying you shouldn't eat anything that you could smell was bad. Dad agreed with Mom. So Wilson figured he better just leave his dinner alone.

"Come on, Wilson. Just one spoonful," Brother Eubieus begged him at first. But then he gave up.

Wilson turned his head just as Brother Eubieus entered the brothers' and nuns' dining room. He caught a whiff of roast chicken, or maybe turkey, being served to them. Their supper smelled good enough to eat.

It was always noisy at mealtimes, but today was worse than usual. Nelson and two big boys were arguing at the end of the next row of tables. Their voices got louder and louder. Then Nelson threw his plate of potatoes and gravy across the table. The plate hit a boy on the side of his head and fell to the floor, leaving gooey mashed potatoes dripping down his face. Just as the boy reached for his plate to fire back, Brother Jerry came marching into the hall.

Nelson slumped down onto the bench. He pulled his cup in front of him and began drinking innocently, watching Brother Jerry out of the corner of his eye. Brother Jerry's face was as red as a beet. His head swivelled back and forth like a tetherball as he tried to figure out what was going on.

All the boys sat perfectly still. Suddenly the room was quiet.

Brother Jerry looked at the food dripping down the boy's face. Then he glared over at Nelson. Wilson held his breath.

"You!" Brother Jerry screamed, pointing at the boy with the potato face. "You get over here." Then he swung around and pointed at Nelson.

"And you!"

Nelson didn't move.

"And you!" Brother Jerry screamed louder. "Get over here before I come and get you myself."

Sullenly Nelson stood up. He didn't say a word. He just glared at Brother Jerry and walked across the room. He didn't take his eyes off the man for an instant.

Wilson waited for Nelson to explode. But Nelson just glared. Brother Jerry wanted a fight, but Nelson wasn't going to give him one. Not today.

"Get out of here! And don't come back until tomorrow.

Neither one of you. Maybe you will be hungry by then."

The two boys walked out. The hall was quiet—at least for a few minutes. Wilson got up and emptied the contents of his plate into the garbage. Then he set the plate on the tray along with his knife and fork, although they weren't dirty.

It wasn't long before Billy Richard figured out that Wilson wasn't eating his food. After that he made sure he sat next to Wilson every meal.

"Hey there, skinny. Where are you from?" Billy said cheerfully as he sat down beside Wilson. "I'm Billy. Billy Richard from Chemainus. My grandfather is the Chief there. What about you?"

Wilson didn't figure what Billy wanted right away, but it didn't take him long to find out.

Billy kept an eye on Wilson's plate of rice and stew as he devoured his own.

"You gonna be eating that food?" he asked.

"Probably not," Wilson answered.

"Wanna work out a deal?"

"What kinda deal?"

"You're a pretty wimpy-looking kid, I figure."

"What about it?" Wilson didn't like where the conversation was going.

"How about a trade?"

"What do you mean?" Wilson was confused. "Trade what?"

"You give me your food. I protect you. Make sure none of these morons rough you up."

"Haven't been roughed up yet." Wilson couldn't see what was in it for him.

"Doesn't mean they ain't gonna start."

That worried Wilson—thinking about getting roughed up. Even Nelson had left him alone since he got to Kuper. He wanted it to stay that way. Maybe a deal with Billy wouldn't hurt. It wasn't like he was going to be eating his food anyway.

After that day, Billy finished his own meal then wolfed down most of Wilson's. Sometimes Wilson tried to eat a few potatoes or a slice of bread—especially when Brother Eubieus came over to help. But there was a knot in his stomach that wouldn't loosen up. His lips were parched, his teeth wouldn't chew and his throat wouldn't swallow.

Bedtime became the best time of day—at least for the first month or so. Every night Wilson and Joey climbed into their own beds. Then, as soon as Brother Eubieus turned out the light, Joey would jump up and leap across into Wilson's bed. He'd snuggle up beside his brother just like he did at home.

Wilson would lie in bed and listen to Joey's gentle breathing. Joey's body would warm up the bed so Wilson felt familiar and safe. He'd watch the moonlight cast long distorted shadows against the wall, and listen to the train whistle and echo across the water from Chemainus, reminding him of home. As sleep overtook him, he would dream of sitting in the kitchen next to the wood stove. Mom would be cooking applesauce and Dad would lay strips of smoked salmon on the table. Then Wilson would rip off a strip of the leathery treat and bite into the chewy fish flesh. The scent of salt mixed with alder would be intoxicating and he'd float weightlessly and be happy.

Wilson made sure he was the first awake in the morning. He'd lie still for a few warm moments then push Joey.

"Come on, Joey. Wake up. You gotta get back into your own bed."

Poor Joey. He had to climb back into his cold bed every

morning so Brother Eubieus wouldn't find out they were sleeping together.

4

ONE NIGHT IN LATE OCTOBER, WILSON WOKE UP. STARTLED, he propped himself up and saw, in light of the moon, Father Maynard and Brother Eubieus leaning over his bed. Father Maynard shoved Joey as he lay next to Wilson.

"What's going on? You have your own beds. Now get out of here." He yanked Joey up and threw him over onto his cold bed. Joey scampered into the bed, pulled the blanket over his head and shivered.

Father Maynard turned to Brother Eubieus. "This is strictly against the rules. I don't want this happening again. I will check these beds every night myself if I have to." With that he left the room.

Brother Eubieus leaned down. "Wilson," he said softly. "I am so sorry. I didn't know he came in and checked. We'd better be careful. Joey?" He pulled the corner of the blanket back from Joey's face. "You have to stay in your own bed. At least for a few nights."

After Brother Eubieus left, Wilson lay in his empty bed with his eyes shut tight. He listened to the other boys wheezing and snoring. He moved his head to the edge of the bed, but he couldn't hear Joey breathe.

Wilson lay still. His bed was cold. Pretty soon he was freezing. He turned over and over, trying to warm up the blankets, but it just got colder and colder without Joey there.

No matter how hard he tried, he couldn't get to sleep. Suddenly he had an uncontrollable urge to pee. He looked for the door, which led to the washroom. The moon had disappeared and the door was hidden in black shadows so Wilson couldn't tell exactly where it was. He lay frozen from cold and fear and began to shiver. He couldn't hold it. Soon he felt warm pee puddle under his bottom and down his legs, soaking his pajamas and blankets.

Wilson remembered the last time he peed the bed. Dad had just moved the outhouse to the edge of the field, way out behind the smokehouse on the other side of the giant oak. It was pitch black out that night and the moon cast no light into the boys' bedroom. He was afraid he would lose his way in the dark, so he lay in bed for too long. Pretty soon he peed. In the morning Mom took the blankets off the bed and hung them on the line to dry.

"Wilson," Mom said sternly, "you make so much work for me. You are too big to pee your bed. You can make it to the outhouse. Now help me lift this mattress to air out."

Wilson was embarrassed. He struggled with Mom to lift the mattress and decided he would never wait too long again. But tonight, as he lay in his bed in the cold, wet blankets, he began to worry about what Brother Eubieus would do in the morning.

As the other boys started getting up, Wilson pulled up his blankets, tucked them tightly under his chin and lay still.

"Up you get," Brother Eubieus called out from the other side of the room. "Come on, Wilson. Time to get out of that bed."

Wilson didn't move. He tried to think of a way to get out of bed without Brother Eubieus finding his wet blankets. But he couldn't. Just as he decided he should get up and make a run for the washroom, Brother Jerry came into the dorm. He looked down the row of beds and saw Wilson tucked under his blankets.

"What do we have here?" he called out. "Got one sleeping in, do you, Brother Eubieus?"

"You afraid to get up, boy?" Brother Jerry let out a mean laugh. "And I bet I know why you're afraid."

Brother Jerry walked across the room and stood right beside the boy's bed. He grabbed the blankets out of Wilson's hands and yanked them back. Wilson shivered in the wet bed.

"Well, look here, boys," Brother Jerry called. "Look what we have. Wilson wants to stay in bed all day and enjoy his wet puddle. Wilson, let me show you what we do with boys who pee their beds at Kuper Island."

A few of the boys gathered around Wilson's bed and snickered. The others ignored Brother Jerry and tried not to watch. They knew what was coming next.

Wilson's body shook involuntarily. A thick, fuzzy sound filled his head while black spots blinded his vision.

"Get up!" Brother Jerry shouted. "Don't just lie there like a fool, boy. Get up and pick up those wet blankets. Take off those stinky pajamas and throw them into the laundry bin."

Brother Eubieus joined Brother Jerry as Wilson swung his legs onto the floor and fumbled with his pajamas.

"I'll take care of this." Brother Eubieus moved to help Wilson.

"I don't need any help," Brother Jerry said sharply. "I've taken care of dozens of boys who pee their beds. Maybe you'll learn a few things if you watch."

Finally Wilson stripped off his pajamas. Naked, he stood paralyzed next to the bed.

"Get the wet laundry, boy," Brother Jerry prodded him. In a daze Wilson did as he was told and threw the blanket into the laundry bin.

"Let's go." Brother Jerry pushed Wilson toward the door. "Okay, boys, we got a cold shower to watch."

Wilson ran ahead to the showers, followed by Brother Jerry and the boys, whose laughter and taunts got louder and louder. Boys from other dorms heard the ruckus and joined the group as they filed down the hall.

"For those who haven't seen it, this is what happens to boys who pee their beds. Take a good look." Brother Jerry turned on the cold water and pushed Wilson in. Wilson squeezed his eyes shut. He didn't want to see Thomas or Joey. He especially didn't want to see Nelson.

Brother Jerry finally turned off the shower, threw Wilson a towel and shoved him out the door. The crowd of laughing boys moved off. Brother Eubieus met him at the dorm.

"Wilson. I am sorry. I went to Father Maynard to try to stop Brother Jerry, but he said that's what they do here at Kuper. Here, let me dry you off. You must be freezing."

Brother Eubieus rubbed the little boy to try to warm his frozen body. Wilson's lips were blue and his teeth chattered. He wanted to thank Brother Eubieus, but he couldn't get warm enough to say a word.

"If you ever wet the bed again, tell me," Brother Eubieus advised. "I won't let this happen again."

Wilson was glad that at least Brother Eubieus hadn't seen him humiliated in the shower.

Brother Eubieus helped him dress and put on a warm sweater. His body shook through breakfast, and he couldn't stop shivering during his first class. He tried to listen to Brother Eubieus and he tried to write the words from the blackboard. The pencil kept falling out of his hand. . . .

Wilson saw Brother Eubieus standing at the front of the class, but he looked fuzzy and distorted. Soon he couldn't see through the heavy spots blocking his sight. The room began to twirl around and around and around. . . .

The next thing Wilson knew he was lying in bed, in a little room. Everything in the room was white, and it was quiet. A boy stood beside the bed.

"Hi, I'm Sammy," he said when Wilson opened his eyes. "They say you passed out in class. You look pretty sick, you know. What's wrong with you?"

Wilson tried to speak, but nothing came out. Soon he fell asleep. Time came and went, but he had no sense of it. Nights and days blended together into what seemed like weeks and months. Wilson tossed and turned in fits of dreams and spells of sleeplessness. Sammy changed his sheets and pajamas when Wilson soaked them with sweat—sometimes twice a day.

Wilson lifted his head when Sammy brought him water or chicken broth, but he couldn't swallow the small spoonfuls of liquid that lay in the back of his throat. Sammy wiped his lips with a damp cloth, and Wilson smiled gratefully.

One morning he woke up with enough strength to help Sammy prop a pillow under his head.

"You gotta eat this morning, Wils. I heard they are gonna take you away if you don't eat."

Wilson opened his mouth. The grey mush slid down his throat. He gagged a little, but he let Sammy spoon some more in.

"Good, Wils. Try some more."

They managed two and then three spoons.

"That's all, Sammy. Please. I'm gonna puke."

"You're pretty sick, you know."

Just as Sammy placed the bowl on the table, Father Maynard led a visitor into the room.

"This is Dr. Bernard Douglas," Father Maynard said. "He is going to give you a checkup."

The short, slight man had a young face but was almost totally bald, aside from a bushy, unkempt half-circle of dark hair curling around his ears and over his stiff, white collar. He placed his black leather bag beside the bed and hooked his stethoscope in one ear and then the other. Carefully he lifted Wilson's pajama top and placed the cold metal against the boy's chest.

"And how are we this morning, young man?" The doctor spoke quietly as he concentrated.

Wilson carefully studied the doctor's expression. Dr. Douglas' deep grey eyes darted from Wilson's face to his watch as he held his fingers firmly against the boy's wrist. He turned Wilson over carefully and listened again with his stethoscope, this time placing it on his back.

"In my opinion," the doctor finally said, "this boy is suffering from malnutrition. Actually, he is starving to death. And it is my professional judgment that this could have been avoided if action had been taken sooner."

Father Maynard was red and breathless. For a moment he was speechless.

Dr. Douglas continued, "Do you not feed the children here? And could you not have called me earlier to examine this poor boy?"

The doctor lightly stroked his hand across Wilson's forehead, over his ears and down his neck. "And he has a low-grade fever."

Flabbergasted, Father Maynard wheezed and sputtered anxiously, "Of course we feed the children here at Kuper. You have never been here before, yet you accuse me of starving my students?"

"I accuse you of nothing, Father Maynard. The boy's condition accuses you of it. Now, if you will excuse me I'll prepare to transfer the boy to the hospital in Chemainus."

"And there you will meet Dr. Emery," Father Maynard said angrily. "He will take over Wilson's care from you. Dr. Emery would never make such wild and false accusations. This young man has been nothing but trouble since he arrived. He is as stubborn as a mule."

The doctor ignored Father Maynard and wrapped Wilson in a blanket, lifted him out of the bed and carried him to the boat, then held him during the long trip to the hospital.

5

ONCE THE NURSES SETTLED WILSON IN A BED, DR. DOUGLAS returned with another doctor.

"Wilson," he said, "this is Dr. Emery. He is the doctor for Kuper Island Residential School. He will be caring for you."

After Dr. Emery examined him, Wilson was left alone. But he could hear the men arguing outside the door.

"This boy has an advanced case of malnutrition."

"Father Maynard would not let a student suffer from such a thing."

"I will look into that school and see for myself."

"You will do nothing of the sort. And if you do, you will not practise at this hospital."

Dr. Douglas did not come to visit Wilson again. He overheard the nurses say the bald doctor had moved over to the mainland, somewhere in Vancouver.

Bags filled with clear liquid hung on a hook near Wilson's bed. A long tube fed the liquid into him through a needle stuck in the back of his hand. The nurse taped the needle down and it hurt if he moved his hand. So Wilson lay as still as he could and made sure his arm didn't move at all.

"Well, young man," a cheery nurse said the third morning after Wilson arrived. "Your fever broke last night while you were asleep. I think we are over the worst of this. Now it's time to take this tube out of your arm so you can eat on your own."

For the first time in—Wilson didn't know how long—his ears weren't ringing and his head felt clear. When the nurse helped him to the washroom, he could almost stand up. But when they tried to feed him, he still couldn't chew. He couldn't swallow. He still couldn't eat anything.

Dr. Emery came in. "Young man, if you don't eat, you will starve yourself to death. That is the last thing Father Maynard needs. Now, we are giving you one more day here at the hospital, and then you are going back to the school. If you don't start eating you will be sent home."

Confused and weak, Wilson struggled to understand what Dr. Emery was telling him. He tried the soup at lunch and then the noodles at supper. But he couldn't get anything down. He thought about the scough bread with butter and blackberry jam Mom had prepared for him that last morning. He yearned to sit on Mom's lap and feel her warmth and comfort. But his mind couldn't focus on her face. It wandered off to Sammy, and Brother Eubieus. He tried to remember Thomas and Joey.

He looked up and cringed. Dr. Emery was standing over him, glaring.

"I . . . I'll try to eat. Really," he mumbled.

The doctor listened again to Wilson's chest and back. He held his wrist, checking the second hand on his watch.

"That's all we can do for you. We can't keep you in hospital because you are too stubborn to eat. Tomorrow Nurse Jeanne will be transporting you back to Kuper Island. And I am telling you, boy, if you know what is good for you—you will start eating."

The next morning Nurse Jeanne gave Wilson a sickly-green housecoat to put over his light blue hospital pajamas. She stuck a pair of matching slippers on his feet and bundled him up in blankets. Then they rode the boat back to Kuper Island. Brother Eubieus met them at the wharf and carried Wilson up to the infirmary.

"The boy still won't eat," Nurse Jeanne reported as she followed them into the school. "Dr. Emery recommends you send him home. He said to tell Father Maynard that, if discipline cannot make the boy eat, he should not trouble himself with a problem child like this one."

When the nurse left, Brother Eubieus brought a bowl of chicken soup and placed it on the windowsill. He helped Wilson sit up and propped some pillows behind his back. Then the brother sat on the side of the bed and held a spoonful of soup up to Wilson's mouth.

"Come on, Wilson," he said gently. "Just try a little."

Wilson opened his lips. He would have done anything for Brother Eubieus, but something happened once the food was in his mouth. His throat gagged shut. It was like it had forgotten how to swallow.

"Please don't get mad," Wilson whimpered. "I just can't do it."

"It's okay, Wilson."

Brother Eubieus placed the spoon in the bowl, picked the bowl up and left the room. A few minutes later he returned with Father Maynard.

Father Maynard stood close to the bed on one side, Brother Eubieus on the other. Father Maynard's face wrinkled into a concerned frown.

"Young man, you have put us in a very difficult position.

If you do not start to eat we will be accused of starving you. This school cannot bear this kind of scandal just to cater to your stubbornness."

He stood silent for a moment.

"We do not have the time and patience to deal with this. I've decided to contact your parents and let them know we will return you to them as soon as arrangements can be made."

Brother Eubieus and Father Maynard left Wilson alone lying in his bed. He looked around the room. It didn't look familiar anymore. How much time had he spent in the infirmary? How long had he been at the hospital? Time became a confused haze.

Now he was going home. Going home. It was all he'd thought about since the day Agent Macdonald took them from Tsartlip. Then Wilson thought about Joey. And Thomas. What about them? If they sent him home, he wouldn't see Thomas and Joey again.

Wilson drifted off into a restless sleep.

He counted three nights. Then on the fourth morning, he heard the sound of heavy feet shuffling up the corridor toward the infirmary. Father Maynard opened the door, red-faced and breathless.

"Hurry up, Wilson. We just got word that Agent Macdonald can pick you up in Chemainus if we get you there by eleven o'clock this morning. That's less than two hours from now. Get your things ready. Jim is on his way with the boat."

Father Maynard left the room as quickly as he'd entered.

Wilson looked around the sterile room. A small pile of clothes was neatly folded on the shelf next to the medicine cabinet. He recognized his own thick, dark brown corduroy pants and his green-striped flannel shirt. They were the clothes he had been wearing the day he got taken away. Even his worn-out shoes sat side by side with their scuffed toes and frayed laces. His old red socks were neatly tucked inside each shoe.

Wilson gingerly twisted his body and dropped his legs over the side of the bed. Turning over, he slowly lowered himself until his toes touched the cold floor. The only time he had walked on his own since he got sick was just two steps to the commode waiting beside his bed and then back again.

He held on to the bedside table and then shuffled to the visitor's chair just steps away from his waiting clothes. His legs wobbled dangerously under the weight of his frail body. He stepped once . . . twice . . . and reached out for his clothes. Then he sank into the chair to dress.

Wilson slipped off his pajama pants and looked down at his brown legs. He didn't remember his knees sticking out or his hip bones being so sharp.

He pulled on his pants and slipped his belt through the loops. His pants hung, just saved from falling on the floor by his hip bones. He yanked the belt tight, but it wasn't tight enough. The last buckle hole was still too loose.

When he finally finished dressing, Wilson sat exhausted on the chair and waited for Father Maynard. He hoped that Brother Eubleus would come and visit him.

If I had any strength in my legs, he thought, I'd open the door and go find Brother Eubieus and Thomas and Joey. But he just sat and waited.

Soon Father Maynard returned.

"Ready to go?"

"Yes."

Father Maynard wrapped Wilson in a blanket and carried him down the hall and outdoors. Wilson squinted in the sunlight. The air was cold against his forehead. But he couldn't see very much. His face was mostly covered by the blanket. And he couldn't move—his arms were stuck against his body. Only his legs hung loose.

Maybe Father Maynard didn't want anyone to see him.

Wilson was glad he couldn't see the school, but he wished he could see Brother Eubieus. Maybe he was waving goodbye from the window. And Joey and Thomas—were they waving goodbye?

Father Maynard huffed and puffed all the way to the boat. Then he breathed a loud, congested sigh of relief as he passed Wilson to Jim the boatman.

"Got one to return, do you?" Jim asked cheerfully.

The boatman took Wilson and laid him down on the hard wooden bench in the cabin. Wilson remembered sitting there the first time, next to Thomas, wishing he was going home. He tried to be happy.

Then he was in his mother's arms. She was rocking him, singing a lullaby.

One morning, two weeks later, Dad burst into the kitchen. Wilson was sitting in a chair, watching Mom peel apples.

"Look, Priscilla," he said. "Look, son. Can you beat this? We got a card in the mail from the Kuper Island Residential School."

Mom looked at the card, glanced at Dad, then passed it to Wilson. He stared at the picture of the giant brick building looming over the bay, the huge evergreens lining the pathway. It all felt like a dream. A bad dream.

Dad turned the card over and read the words.

Dear Mr. and Mrs. Jones,

We regret to inform you that your son Wilson has fallen sick. Please be prepared for him to return home to your care. You should be expecting him any day.

We believe he was taken too young from his mother. He refused to eat and could not build up his strength to fight off the influenza. We took every precaution and provided all the medical care we could, including sending him to the hospital in Chemainus. They were unable to find a remedy. And we regret that we were unable to administer a cure.

In our judgment, Wilson will be better cared for by his mother.

His personal possessions are being returned with him. Please do not send him back to the school until he is fully recovered.

Sincerely,
Father Maynard

ps Thomas and Joey are doing well. They will remain at the school.

Joey

1

"JOEY!" THOMAS GRABBED HIS ARM. HIS OLDER BROTHER was out of breath. "Have you seen Wils?"

"No." Joey shrugged. "I haven't seen him forever. I'm not allowed to visit him. Brother Eubieus says."

"No, Joey. I mean have you seen him this morning? I heard Father Maynard talking to Agent Macdonald on the phone. He said Jim is picking up Wils before lunch. Be on the lookout. Maybe we can see him before he goes."

Joey leaned heavily against the wall in disbelief. Wilson was going home.

Joey straightened up and ran down the stairs. He had to find Brother Eubieus. Brother Eubieus had to send him home with Wilson.

He found the teacher in the dining room. Brother Eubieus looked tired and angry. His lips were white, with only a hint of colour around the edges.

"Brother Eubieus. Please," Joey begged, "I have to go home with Wils. I have to."

"No, Joey. You can't. And who told you Wilson was going home, anyway?"

"Please! Please! Wils will need me to look after him on the trip."

"Joey." Brother Eubieus looked stern. "You go to the dorm and don't come out until I say. You are not going home with Wilson, and that is it."

In despair, Joey turned and slowly headed up the stairs. When he reached the dorm, he sat in the corner of the deep windowsill, arms curled around his legs, and gazed listlessly over the bay and off into the distant mountains.

Suddenly, between the trees, he saw Father Maynard hustling down the path in front of the school. He had something wrapped up like a baby in his arms. Father Maynard's body jerked awkwardly back and forth as he hurried along. It looked like he was trying to get rid of something dangerous.

It had to be Wilson. But the child that hung limp over the father's arms didn't look big enough to be Wilson. Joey trained his eyes on the blanket. He caught a glimpse of his brother's shoes—at the ends of thin, pale legs, which swung aimlessly. He looked closer to make sure. It was Wilson. Why wasn't he walking?

Father Maynard passed Wilson to Jim, who disappeared with him into the cabin. The priest wiped his hands on his black gown, straightened out the creases and when Jim reappeared, shook the boatman's hand before waddling back up the wharf.

Soon a large puff of blue smoke billowed from the engine, and the boat headed out into the bay. Joey stared at the craft until it shrank into a speck and disappeared into the grey haze hanging over Chemainus.

He thought about Mom and Dad and Roger and the twins waiting at the top of the path for Wilson to arrive with Agent Macdonald. Mom would be so happy. She would pick Wilson up and hug him. She would take him into the kitchen and make hot tea. She would find him a piece of scough bread left over from breakfast, and maybe she would spread some butter and blackberry jam on the bread for a treat.

If he had gone home with Wilson, Mom would pick him up too, and hold him and kiss his face. She would kiss him again and again, hugging so tight, his ribs would hurt. Joey squeezed his eyes shut and sucked in a deep breath. For that moment he was home in Mom's arms.

He was startled when he opened his eyes. Brother Eubieus sat next to him on the windowsill.

"I am sorry," Brother Eubieus said. "I am so sorry that you couldn't see Wilson before he left. But Father Maynard wouldn't even let me see him. He hasn't let me visit Wilson for days."

Brother Eubieus picked Joey up and placed him on his knee. They sat quietly together for a time. Brother Eubieus hugged him tightly, then, without a word, set him back on the windowsill and left the room.

Joey watched Brother Eubieus leave. Now, he felt all alone. The school had changed his mind about a lot of things. The ride in the big, black car hadn't turned out to be as much fun as he had expected. The boat ride over hadn't been much fun either. By the time Joey had arrived at the school the first day, he was feeling sick to his stomach and starving. He still felt the same. He should have run home from the Day School when Thomas told him to. He never should have swung on the door of that car.

He looked around the dorm. He examined each bed lined up in its row, wrapped tightly in faded yellow blankets. The floor was so shiny you could slide from one end of the room to the other, if no one was in your way. Joey scanned the floor. Just like on the day he arrived, there wasn't a toy or a paper or a sock or shoe anywhere. If you bent down and looked under the beds, you could see right across the room under every bed, right to the other wall, not one thing stopping you. Nothing.

No one kicked their shoes under their beds or stashed their junk in piles. No one hid their stuff down there. In fact, there wasn't much of anything in the room. Just him.

A lump rose in his throat. There was a knot in his stomach. His eyes stung as warm salty tears welled up. Then angrily he wiped his eyes and nose on his sleeve and jumped down from the windowsill. I'm getting off this stupid island too, he decided. I am going to make a plan, and I am going home.

Working out a plan wasn't easy. He thought of swimming across to Chemainus, but it was too far. He thought of sneaking a ride on Jim's boat, but Jim's boat was too small to hide in. Jim would find him easily and send him back.

Joey thought of starving himself so he got sick like Wilson. But it didn't matter how bad the meat loaf or morning mush tasted, he was ravenous. He ate every bite.

One of his best plans was to escape on the old barge that came across to the island to deliver supplies. Joey thought

he would sneak down to the end of the wharf, then swim to the far side of the barge and climb in. Then he would hide in an empty container and ride to Chemainus. But he couldn't figure out how to get home from Chemainus. He was only five.

He worked on one escape plan after the other. But with each plan came another problem he couldn't quite figure out. Weeks passed and he still didn't have a plan that would work.

Then months passed. . . .

Then years.

2

It was late October, just after Joey's birthday. Birthdays weren't any real big thing on Kuper, but Mom had sent him a card. It arrived right on the October 24th. Mom did it every year. Somehow she knew how to make sure the mail arrived right on his birthday.

This year, Joey's tenth birthday had been observed by the school. He was transferred from Brother Eubieus' dorm to Brother Henry Philipe's. He lay on his bed in the corner, contemplating his birthday card. On the front there was a picture of a small boy in short pants. He had a chubby pink face and was holding a fishing line. *Happy Birthday, Son* framed the picture in gold-embossed letters. He knew Mom considered every card on the metal rack at the grocery store before choosing the perfect one.

Inside the verse read:

> *By a little bird I was told*
> *The Birthday Boy is 10 years old*
> *Just a little card to say*
> *Have a very perfect day*

Joey didn't pay much attention to the words of the verse. He gently touched the card and ran his hand over Mom's message on the bottom, printed in large, deliberate letters.

My dear Joey
I miss you so much. I love you and am proud of you. Be good at school. Happy Birthday, son.
Love Mom and Dad and the kids.
XOXOXOXOXOXO

He thought of Mom struggling to write the message. He saw Dad printing the words so Mom could copy them letter by letter with her own hand. He thought of how Mom wished she knew how to read and write properly. He felt an overwhelming love for Mom. He wanted to hug her and tell her how much he missed her. Dad too. And the kids.

He pressed the card to his chest and lay back on his bed. Just as he closed his eyes, Brother Henry Philipe came into the room.

"Joey," Brother Henry Philipe said, "I want you to meet Harvey Dennis. He will be sleeping in the bed right next to yours. I want you to show him around."

Joey sat up. Standing next to the brother was the shortest boy he had ever seen. He was short enough to be only five or six years old, but he looked older. He had thick, densely matted hair that seemed glued together in sticky clumps, randomly poking up. He hadn't had a bath in weeks, Joey thought. His hands were black with dirt packed under his fingernails. Joey could smell a repugnant odour of smoke and sweat and mildew coming from the boy.

His shirt sleeves sagged over his wrists even though they were folded several times into a thick roll. His pant legs were shredded at the bottom and they dragged on the floor, covering his shoes.

Joey stared at the wretched-looking boy.

"What's your name?" the boy said quickly.

"I'm Joey. And if you're gonna sleep next to me, you better not snore all night, Stumpy."

"My name is Harvey Dennis," he snapped.

"Yeh, I heard. What's with your legs? Did someone cut you off at the knees?" Joey snickered.

Stumpy fired an annoyed look back at Joey as he threw his jacket on the bed.

"There is no need for names, Joey," Brother Henry Philipe butted in. "Harvey is short for his age, but he's older than you. He's eleven. I want you to make him feel at home."

Brother Henry Philipe pulled Stumpy over to the clothes

bin and began rummaging through it.

"Here," Brother Henry Philipe said. "Now take a shower, put these on and throw your old clothes in the garbage can. Then we'll cut your hair and give your hands an extra scrub," he added in disgust.

Joey dozed off until Stumpy returned. Now his hair was cut short across the top and up the sides like everyone else's. His hands were clean except for a little dirt still caked under his nails. A thick, black belt was wrapped several times around his waist, holding his shirt in and his pants up. But his pant legs still dragged along on the floor behind him.

Stumpy shuffled over to his bed, shoes flapping with each step. Then he lay on the bed, shoes and all.

"Hi," he said.

"Hi."

Joey scanned the small boy. His shoes poked up comically, as if they belonged to another body.

"I can help you with those shoes. I used to have the same trouble back at home when I was small. I always wore my older brother's hand-me-downs. His name is Thomas. Whenever I got a pair of his shoes, Mom stuffed the ends with old socks. Worked pretty good. Keeps you from having to shuffle around, trying to hold on to your shoes with your toes curled up."

"Yeh, thanks."

"We can use toilet paper from the can and stuff the ends."

"They couldn't find any shoes small enough." Stumpy gazed up at the ceiling.

"Let's go, then," Joey said.

Stumpy followed Joey into the washroom. Joey pulled off a handful of toilet tissue and scrunched it up into two balls. Then he stuffed them into the toes of Stumpy's shoes.

"How about that?"

Stumpy walked a few steps.

"Pretty good."

Joey showed Stumpy around the school. After supper they returned to the dorm and flopped on their beds.

"How come they threw you in here, Stumpy?" Joey asked.

There was a long silence.

"I guess they think my grandpa is too old to look after me. The government agent came around the other day when I was fixing supper for Gramps. He said they were taking me to school. Gramps didn't understand one word the agent was saying, but I did."

"So what happened?"

"Yesterday I stayed home from the Day School because Gramps wasn't feeling so good. Then the guy came back."

Stumpy hesitated and a heavy sadness filled his face. Joey waited for him to continue, but Stumpy remained silent. Joey figured out the rest of the story.

"It's not that bad here, really."

"That's not what I hear. Feels like they just threw me in jail."

Joey shrugged. "You learn how to get by. In class it's easy. The brothers don't teach you much, but you have to look like you're paying attention. If you're caught looking out the window, you're gonna get the ruler."

"The ruler?" Stumpy asked.

"Yeh, it's not so bad. If you talk back, you're sent to Father Maynard. He's got a leather strap. That can really hurt."

Stumpy shuddered. "Anyone ever escape from this place?"

"My brother Wils got sick so they sent him home a few years ago. And a few kids have tried to escape. I heard Truman Neilson got home. Then there were the Barry sisters. They tried to get away in a canoe. One came back. They say the other one drowned, but no one talks about it much."

"Where you from, Joey?"

"Tsartlip, down by Victoria. What about you?"

"Hey, we are just about neighbours. I'm from Pauquachin, just up the road. That's where my grampa lives and all my aunts and uncles and cousins. Ever heard of Gramps? His name is Abel Dennis."

"I don't think so," Joey replied. His answer made him feel sad. "I've been in this place since I was five years old. I go home in the summer for a bit and I got to go home last Christmas. But there are lots of people I don't know. Lots I've forgotten. My brother Thomas is here. It's not so bad. I got family. I got a few cousins here too."

"Well, I'm not staying around long enough to forget who lives at home," Stumpy said with determination. "Gramps is waiting for me. When that agent pushed me out the door, I called back to Gramps and told him that I'd be right home to look after him. That's what I'm going to do, Joey. I'm going to go home to look after Gramps."

The two boys were silent. Soon Joey's old plans flooded into his mind. He thought of escaping on the barge, stealing a canoe, sneaking a ride on Jim's boat.

"I guess you've never thought of running away, eh, Joey?"

What did Stumpy think? That he was the first person to think of escaping?

"Every day," Joey retorted. Then, all of a sudden, his anger dissolved. He looked over at Stumpy. Of course! That was why Stumpy was here and was given the bed next to his. Joey's mind was clear. The voice inside him screamed, *You can do it, Joey. You* and *Stumpy.*

He sat up.

"You know what Dad tells me every summer when I go

home? He tells me that everything happens for a reason. He says that sometimes you don't know what the reason is, and sometimes it looks like there is no good reason. But there is always a reason. Well, I just figured it out."

He lay back and shut his eyes.

"Figured *what* out?"

Joey rolled over and whispered deliberately, "Stumpy. Listen to me. I have been working on plans to escape from this place for years. Ever since Wils was shipped out of here, I've tried to figure out how to get back home—to stay. Now you're here. And you get the bed right next to me. And you want to escape too."

Stumpy considered the idea for a moment.

Joey continued. "What I need to know is . . . are you serious?"

Stumpy leaned over furtively and replied, "Yeh, I'm serious. I ain't never been serious like this in my whole life."

Joey nodded. "Things work out even when you don't see it coming."

Joey and Stumpy never noticed the other boys getting ready for bed or the room growing dark. Heads together, they worked on a plan.

It didn't take the boys long to agree on their method of escape to Chemainus. After weighing all the pros and cons of hiding on the barge or on Jim's boat, they decided it was better to sneak onto one of the fish boats that tied up at the wharf from time to time. They figured they could hide until the boat reached Chemainus or Duncan and then make a run for it.

But how would they get home from there?

"That's the easy part," Joey said at last. "We can walk. We won't get lost if we follow the train tracks. They'll lead us into Victoria. From there, we can find someone we know. Or we can walk, 'cause I know the way."

Stumpy's eyes closed. He lowered his head onto the pillow.

"What's wrong with you, Stumpy? I thought you were into it. You got a problem with walking? We've got lots of time. It's not like we got a bus to catch."

"Yeh, right, Joey. I got no problem with walking. I could keep up to you any day."

It took a few days before Joey found out what Stumpy was worried about. One night, after the lights were out and the boys had finished planning for the evening, Stumpy leaned over towards Joey's bed.

"Joey," he whispered. "You still awake?"

"Yeh. What's up?"

"I'm afraid of bears."

"What?"

"I'm afraid of bears. And cougars."

"What are you telling me for? Do you think they're hiding under the bed?"

"No. I'm afraid to walk home along the train tracks. It's the woods the whole way. There are gonna be bears and cougars up there."

Joey leaned towards Stumpy. "So that's your problem. Well, what else can we do? It's not like we can walk right down the road. We'd be picked up by the police. Then what would we say? 'Geez, officer, we were just out for a walk. Thanks for asking.'"

"Lay off, Joey," Stumpy grumbled. "I'm telling you, I'm scareder than a baby of wild animals. I heard there are cougars and bears all over the place. Bobcats and raccoons, too. And what about if we run into a bat? You know they can smother you with their wings?"

If their escape plan was going to work, Joey knew he'd better take Stumpy seriously.

"Hey," Joey said confidently. "You are safe with me. I'm used to the woods. Dad takes me hunting in the summer. I know what to do."

He wished it were true. He had been hunting only once with Dad and Thomas. He tried to remember Dad's teachings.

"Dad says we got nothing to worry about in the woods. If you respect the animals they will respect you. Dad said, once him and Uncle Shorty were hunting up on Willis Point when they came across a black bear. Or it came across them. The bear was standing five steps from Dad. It was almost as tall as him, too. Dad says, the thing about black bears is that they know when they've met their match. And there is nothing like a good Indian to be a match for a black bear. So there they stood. Face to face. Eye to eye. 'Joey,' Dad says, 'the worst thing is not looking into the eye of a black bear, it's that black bear looking right back in your eye. He is looking right into your heart—into the sort of man that you are.' Dad had two choices. Shoot that son of a gun dead in one shot, or stare him down until he walked away."

Stumpy's eyes were as big as moons. Joey waited.

"Yeh, Joey? Is that true?" Stumpy gasped. "Did your dad really stand eye to eye with a black bear?"

"It's the full truth, Stumpy. Just like Dad tells it. And at this point in the story Dad always waits a while. Then he looks me right in the eye and goes on.

"'That black bear,' Dad says, 'looked so far down into my heart, he looked right through me.' That's when Dad knew he didn't have to shoot the bear. They had an agreement, Dad and the bear. The black bear turned around on his hind legs and took off through the underbrush. And that's Dad's story, Stumpy. Just like he tells it."

"You think it's true, Joey? You think wild animals would just walk away from us if we stared them down?"

"I know one thing for sure, Stumpy. I never saw the hide of no black bear hanging around our house and I know for sure he never got Dad's hide. So they must have made some kinda deal."

The story seemed to help. Stumpy didn't talk about wild animals much after that.

3

NIGHT AFTER NIGHT STUMPY AND JOEY WHISPERED BACK and forth, perfecting the plan.

"Now all we need is the fish boat and we're set," Joey said one night. "Keep an eye out."

A few weeks later, three fish boats tied up to the wharf. The next day Stumpy looked out the window.

"There are still two boats tied up," he said. "They'll probably take off for Chemainus early tomorrow morning."

"That means our plan is a go," Joey replied. "This evening we'll collect the food. Then, when everyone is asleep, we'll sneak out the back door and go around to the wharf and down to the fish boat. We'll hide out in the fish hold until Chemainus. Got it, Stumpy?"

"Got it, Joey," Stumpy said with a salute. They were ready.

When they arrived in the dining hall for lunch, everybody was talking.

"Did you hear about Harry Tommy and Nick Herman?" said Billy. "They're missing in action. Since last night. Brother Jerry checked the beds at four o'clock this morning and they were gone." Billy George always had the news on everything.

"What do you mean—missing?" Stumpy looked dumbfounded.

"I mean gone—as in not there," Billy replied. "Gone, as in

they got out of here. I hear they jumped on one of the fish boats for a free ride to Chemainus. I sure hope they don't get caught, that's all."

"Ahem. Ahem." Brother Jerry stood in the centre of the room.

Everyone kept talking until he shouted, "Shut up! You boys shut up and listen!"

Suddenly the room was quiet. All eyes turned toward Brother Jerry.

"Harold Tommy and Nicholas Herman have run away. And I know some of you boys, sitting here right now, know where they are. I am not going to waste my time looking for them. I am going to stand right here and wait for one of you to step up and tell me where they are."

"He is going to stand there for a long time," Joey whispered to Stumpy.

The senior boys hung their heads to avoid Brother Jerry's piercing stare.

"Sure as anything, every one of the seniors knows what happened," Stumpy whispered back.

"If no one comes up and tells the truth . . ." Brother Jerry couldn't stand still. He paced back and forth across the room tapping his foot up and down like he was performing some kind of chicken dance. ". . . if you all sit there like dummies, then each and every one of you will get a beating until I find out. If I haven't heard anything by two o'clock, then two boys will be chosen and they will get the belt. And if that doesn't work, there will be two more with the belt by supper."

No one needed to tell anything. And no one got the belt except for Harry and Nick. By afternoon class everyone knew the story.

"They got caught," Billy George announced as he ran breathless into the classroom. "Once they got over to Chemainus the fisherman caught them crouched down in the corner of the cabin of the boat. As soon as the guy saw them he turned his boat right around and brought them back to the school. He took Nick and Harry by their ears and dragged them up the wharf and straight to Father Maynard's office."

Within minutes everyone could hear the belt.

Slap. Crack. Bang.

Over and over they heard the sound of leather meeting flesh.

Everyone could hear Father Maynard and Brother Jerry shouting, but Nick and Harry were silent. Finally the beating subsided.

That night Stumpy whispered, "I don't think escaping from this place is such a good idea, Joey."

It was quiet in the dorm, but Joey could still hear the sound of the odd blanket shuffling as someone turned over. "Maybe later, Stumpy. It's not safe right now."

They listened to the sound of the dark room. Other than the groan and hiss of the old radiators, it was silent. No one was snoring or snorting. Maybe everyone was holding their breath, thinking of the sound from Father Maynard's office.

Joey lay there, barely breathing. He was trapped, cornered on that God-awful island, with no way off. He listened as, one by one, the boys' breathing grew heavy. Stumpy finally began to snore. Off in the distance, Joey could hear the whistle of the train winding its way south from Chemainus to Victoria.

The boys didn't talk about escaping again until months later, one morning in early March.

"Joey," Stumpy asked, "do you think that we will ever get off this island?"

"'Course we will, Stumpy." Joey had almost given up hope.

But he wasn't going to tell Stumpy.

"Yeh, right, Joey. I mean are we *really* going to do it? I heard that Gramps is sick. My cousin Lucas wrote to me. He said they took Gramps to the hospital and he might not come home."

A few days after Stumpy got the news about his grandfather, the boys started planning again.

It started with Telford Lewis. Telford was a chubby, short kid who arrived from the mainland and was assigned the bed next to Stumpy.

Joey and Stumpy ignored Telford until bedtime. The new boy cried when he heard the train whistle, then he sobbed and wiped his nose noisily on his blanket.

"Telford," Joey said quietly. "Two things you gotta know about Kuper. Don't cry all night and don't pee your bed."

It didn't help. The third night Telford lay huddled up in his bed as Joey and Stumpy listened to him snivel and wipe his nose. Soon Telford began crying out loud.

"What's wrong now, Telford?" Stumpy said.

"I peed my bed. It's wet. I'm cold," he whimpered.

"What did we tell you, stupid?" Joey said.

"If you pee your bed they'll make you parade around in your bare butt. Geez, Telford," Stumpy added in disgust. "We're gonna have to watch the shower parade tomorrow, and then we'll have to protect you from the seniors. Why'd you have to pee? You stupid?"

Joey remembered the morning Brother Jerry had hauled Wilson down to the shower. He thought about Moses, Clifford and the other boys who'd wet their beds. He didn't want to watch the same thing happen to Telford.

But it was Stumpy who got up. He rummaged through the laundry pile and pulled out some pajamas and a blanket. Joey was just about to warn him to be quiet when—*thump, crash!* —something fell and smashed on the floor.

Stumpy turned and ran toward his bed, but before he got there, light filled the room and Brother Jerry stood in the doorway. Brother Henry Philipe was behind, looking over his shoulder. Stumpy was standing in the middle of the room with a pair of pajamas and a blanket trailing behind him.

"Harvey!" Brother Jerry shouted. "What are you doing up in the middle of the night? What's all this glass on the floor? I want an explanation! I want it now! You are nothing but trouble. I need my sleep. You boys are nothing but wild Indians. . . ."

Brother Jerry wouldn't quit. He carried on ranting. "What do you think you are doing? What's that blanket. . . ?"

All the boys sat up and stared at the brother's rampage. All, that is, except Telford, who tucked his head under his wet blanket, shivering with cold and fear.

Joey watched Stumpy in amazement.

Stumpy turned around and looked straight at Brother Jerry. Any other time the sight of Brother Jerry—his pale blue nightshirt barely covering his knees, his white, hairy legs and long, bony feet—would have made Joey crack up laughing. But everyone's eyes were trained on Stumpy.

"I got up to help Telford change his sheets," Stumpy said slowly and purposefully. "He peed his bed, and I am sick of watching you parade us around like we are a bunch of trained animals. So I got up to change his sheets. Then I bumped the shelf, and that stupid glass jug fell on the floor. And now it's broken all over the place. Why do we have a stupid glass jug on the shelf, anyway? And then you come walking in, dressed in that stupid nightdress, looking like an old woman and screaming like a fool. Why are you awake this time of night? Don't you ever sleep?"

Now it was Stumpy who was carrying on. Stop now, Stumpy, Joey thought. Stop now.

But Stumpy wasn't finished. "And I'm not gonna stand

around, watching Telford's bare butt get a cold shower in the morning while you and the senior boys enjoy yourself. So I'm gonna change his bed."

Brother Jerry shook with rage. His red face looked ready to explode. He took a few steps toward Stumpy before he realized he was in the middle of a pile of glass. Suddenly he was dancing on his tiptoes, shrieking—out of control.

If the boys hadn't been so shocked they would have laughed their guts out. Instead, they sat speechless.

"What are you gonna do about it?" Stumpy asked defiantly.

"What am I going to do about it?" Brother Jerry's voice was high pitched and shrill. "What am I going to do about it? I'll tell you what I'm going to do about it, you dirty little brat. I am going to lock you in the laundry closet for the rest of the night, since you are so interested in the laundry. And you'll stay there without any food until I decide to come and get you. You think you'll be talking so tough after that, mister clean sheets?"

Brother Jerry flashed his eyes, smacked his lips and flapped his arms up and down, slapping his thighs as if he was about to do or say something important. After a few seconds, he charged across the room and grabbed Stumpy. Stumpy kicked and screamed as they disappeared out the door.

Brother Henry Philipe told Telford to get out of bed and change his pajamas and blankets. It was lucky for Telford that Stumpy had made such a big scene. Now all Brother Henry Philipe wanted to do was to clean up and settle everyone down.

"Joey, you get the broom and sweep up this floor. Make sure you don't miss anything."

Stumpy never appeared all the next day. He didn't show up for class that morning, or lunch, or afternoon class. Joey waited for Stumpy in the dining hall at suppertime, but his place sat empty. That evening, just after Brother Henry Philipe turned the lights out, the boys heard Brother Jerry coming down the hall. His voice was loud.

"Harvey," he barked, "get to bed. And I hope you've learned your lesson."

He pushed Stumpy into the dorm and shut the door. Stumpy fumbled around in the darkness until he found his bed.

"Joey," he whispered. "We are going to make plans to get out of here. Tomorrow, you and me, we are going to get off this island. And I am never coming back."

"Where were you?" Joey asked.

"In the laundry closet down by Father Maynard's office. Brother Jerry stuffed me in there last night. I never got anything to eat. They never even opened the door. I heard Brother Jerry tell Father Maynard that they better split us up. We won't get to sleep next to each other anymore, and we won't be able to sit together in class or at meals. They say we're trouble. But we're getting out of here, Joey."

"I got Thomas to sneak some food from the kitchen. In case you came back tonight."

Joey dragged a pillowcase out from his cubbyhole. He pulled out an apple, half a loaf of bread and two cookies. Stumpy gobbled them up.

"I had a lot of time to think in that stupid closet. I think our best plan is to escape by canoe. Tomorrow night, we'll get some food from the kitchen, hide the paddles under the canoe and be ready to go the next morning. We can leave before anyone gets up and paddle to Chemainus before they even know we're gone."

"Hold on, Stumpy," Joey replied. "Nelson already tried that a long time ago with Colin Joe. They stole a canoe and only got as far as Thetis Island before a boat caught up with them and hauled them back. Brother Jerry whipped their butts, worse than Harry and Nick."

"They made mistakes, Joey. They didn't think it out. For one thing, they headed out in the afternoon, and they also told everyone. We'll leave early in the morning and we'll be on the other side of Thetis before anyone wakes up. By the time they come looking for us, we'll be on our way. We can stick close to the shore on Thetis so we can hide if a boat comes after us. And we aren't gonna tell everyone—just the people we need."

"Geez, it sounds like you've thought of everything." Joey was impressed.

"I thought of one more thing. We need a decoy for when they figure out we're missing."

"What do you mean—a decoy?" Joey asked.

"Let's send them looking the wrong way. We know they are going to ask Telford if he heard us talking about running away. So let's get him to say he overheard us planning our escape and that we were going to run to Kuper village. He can tell them that we're going to my Auntie Martha's house. By the time they find out what a liar he is, we'll be in Chemainus. We hit the tracks and they never find us."

"Stumpy, that closet sure changed you into one smart, brave guy."

"Yeh, I thought it out pretty good in there. And another thing—I saved my birthday money and I figure it should get us what we need," Stumpy added. "We can pay Thomas a dollar to get us enough food for the trip—bread and cookies, and maybe apples and a few carrots. We'll have four dollars left for supplies and our trip home. Just in case."

Joey thought about telling Thomas, but he worried that his older brother would try to talk him out of it. Mostly he didn't want to leave Thomas at Kuper all alone.

His excitement turned to fear and sadness when he thought about it.

4

THE NEXT MORNING JOEY WAITED IN THE CORRIDOR AFTER class. He met Thomas leaving his classroom.

"Hey, brother," Thomas said cheerfully as he slapped Joey on the back. "So what's up with you this morning?"

"I need to talk to you, Thomas," Joey said under his breath. "I need to ask you a big favour."

"Of course, little brother, anything."

"No, Thomas, listen to me. We need to talk."

"What's the big secret?" Thomas laughed. "It sounds like you're planning a heist."

"Not really, Thomas. But almost."

Joey pulled Thomas outside the back door of the school and explained the plan.

"We need you to get us some food for the trip. Please, Thomas. We got a dollar for you if you'll do it."

"No, Joey. Don't do it. You know what happened to Harry and Nick and the others, don't you? And you must have heard of the Barry sisters. One of them drowned trying to run away. And even Nelson, he tried it too. Don't do it, Joey. What will Mom say?"

Joey tried to ignore Thomas' questions. "We are going tomorrow whether you help us or not. If we don't get any food, then we'll be hungry. Stumpy and I are running away. We have to, brother, and we need your help."

"Is Telford going for it? Do you think he will do his part?"

"He'll be okay. We've gone over it with him and he knows what he needs to say."

"I am warning you, little brother. You could get into trouble. It might not work like you planned. I don't want you getting hurt."

"Then get us some food. Please, Thomas. 'Cause we are going, with your help or without it."

"I always thought you were crazy, Joey. Now I know."

He gave Joey a friendly cuff up the side of his head. "You got guts, kid. Give Mom and Dad a big hug from me if you make it. And a hug for all the kids."

He pulled open the back door, then said over his shoulder, "I'll see what I can do."

Joey waited for an instant, then followed his brother. "Why don't you come with us? You don't hafta stay here," he said impulsively.

"Yes, I do. I've got used to it here, Joey. It's not so bad. Not for me. The soccer's good. I like being on the team—we're great. Anyway, I just do what I'm told—not like you. But I'm sure gonna miss you."

Joey wasn't surprised. He just wished he didn't have to leave Thomas at Kuper.

That evening Joey and Stumpy made sure they had everything ready. Stumpy sneaked into the tool shed and got three paddles. One for Joey, one for him and one just in case a paddle broke. He ran down to the beach and hid the paddles under the upturned canoe.

Thomas brought them a bag of food after dinner—two loaves of bread, eight cookies, six apples and four carrots.

"That's all I could get," he said briefly, slipping the bag under Joey's coat. Joey took the goods, ran into the dorm and hid the food in a pillowcase. Then the boys stashed their jackets, two sheets and Stumpy's four dollars with the food in their cubbyholes.

When everything was ready the two boys jumped into bed.

"Everything in order, escape buddy Stumpy?" Joey asked quietly.

"Everything in order. I don't think I'm gonna sleep

tonight. My gut hurts." Stumpy laughed nervously.

"One more sleep, and we are out of here," Joey added. He looked around the room, hoping it would be the last time he saw the place. His eyes landed on Telford.

"Telf," Joey whispered. "What are you gonna say when they ask you where we've gone?"

"I know what I gotta say," Telford replied. "I'm gonna tell them that I heard you guys planning to run away to Stumpy's auntie's place in Kuper village."

"You got it, Telf. Thanks for your help."

"I'm gonna miss you guys. Who's gonna sleep in our corner?" Telford started whimpering.

"Don't worry, Telf," Joey answered. "They'll catch some other kids and throw them into our beds. I left you some cookies in your cubbyhole for your trouble."

"Hey, thanks, Joey." Telford perked up. "I'll always remember you guys."

5

JOEY FELT A PUSH ON HIS SHOULDER. "JOEY, JOEY, I'M READY. Let's go."

The room was chilly and still dark. Joey groped around and found his clothes. He slipped his pajamas off and dressed in one minute. He picked up his jacket and the pillowcase.

Stumpy grabbed the sheets and they headed out the door. The hallway was dark and eerie. The stairs creaked as the boys stepped gingerly from one to the other. Moonlight shone out from behind the clouds and cast muted shadows on the walls. Joey caught his breath. For a moment he thought he saw Brother Jerry hiding in a dark corner by the front door.

Outside, the boys ran from bush to bush, making sure they were camouflaged by shadows. When they reached the beach they turned the canoe right side up and quietly placed it into the water.

"Hold on, Stumpy." Joey paused. "My dad taught me never to go in a canoe without asking the Creator for a safe trip."

Stumpy stood still.

"Creator," Joey began. "Could you give us a safe trip? And make sure no one wakes up too early this morning. . . ." He couldn't think of anything more to say, so he bent down to pick up the paddles.

Stumpy stood for a few more seconds. "Is that it?" he asked.

"Yeh, you got anything you want to say?" Joey replied.

"How about something like getting God to make sure we don't get caught or get lost or get eaten or get—"

"All right. Come on. Get in." Joey placed the paddles gently into the bottom of the canoe and held it steady as Stumpy climbed in and balanced himself in the narrow bow of the craft. It wobbled from side to side as Joey stepped in and sat down.

"You ever pulled a canoe before, Stumpy?" Joey asked as the canoe headed one way and then the other, shifting dangerously from side to side.

"Not really," Stumpy admitted. "I forgot to tell you that. How about you?"

"Thanks for telling me now." Joey tried to steady the canoe and guide it toward Thetis Island. "Yeh. I pull in the summer. I compete in the races down the beach," he added proudly. "Last year I got first place in the buckskin division."

"Don't worry about me," Stumpy said confidently. "I'm a quick learner. Just tell me when to switch."

Soon they were gliding gracefully along the beach, paddles in perfect unison. Neither boy spoke. It was silent, apart from the soft *swoosh, swoosh* of their paddles as they gently cut through the water.

"Switch," Joey called ahead to his partner. Both boys pulled their dripping paddles out of the water and passed them over to the other side and continued.

The moon was high, but thick, black clouds partially blocked the light from the travellers. The mill crowding the beach in Chemainus lit the sky, while billows of smoke spewed out of the stacks. Soon the silence was interrupted by a hum from the machines in the mill starting up for the early shift. The sky slowly faded from black to dark grey. Then orange and red streaked across the landscape. A light haze lay over the still waters of the channel.

Joey watched, in amazement, the changing colours across

the sky, the sparkle as light hit the tiny ripples on the water, the birds rustling as they woke up with their first songs and Stumpy and him paddling along the shore on their way to Chemainus. On their way home. It all didn't seem real. Joey stopped himself from thinking about what would happen if someone found them. He felt the air warm slightly as the night turned into morning. He kept his eyes on the mill as a beacon while he steered the canoe past Thetis Island.

"Do you think they're looking for us yet?" Stumpy asked as they neared the Chemainus harbour.

"Yeh, maybe."

They paddled quickly past the wharf. Jim's boat was tied up next to a few salmon trawlers and cabin cruisers. The wharf was sleepy and still. No one in sight. The boys watched the harbour and shore nervously for a sign that anyone might spot them.

"In here," Joey said with authority. He pointed to a small pebbled beach with thick maples and alders leaning over into the water.

"We can pull up the canoe and hide it in the trees. I think the train tracks are just up the hill."

Joey dug his paddle deep into the water and turned the canoe toward the shore. Soon stones were rattling and scraping under the hull.

"Pull it right up, Stumpy," Joey said, not caring about what damage might be caused from the weight of their bodies. "I don't want to get my feet wet."

The bow lifted up onto the dry beach. Stumpy stood up and jumped onto the rocks. Joey picked up the pillowcase and sheets and climbed over Stumpy's seat, then gingerly stepped out of the wobbling craft.

Both boys hesitated for a few moments to stretch their cramped legs.

"Look!" Stumpy exclaimed. He pointed up into the sky.

"Wow! It's gonna be a good day," Joey commented, as he stood for a few moments and watched a young eagle soaring in wide circles over the place where they'd landed. "Dad says that when an eagle circles over you things are gonna be okay."

They left the canoe and paddles hidden in the trees by the beach, headed into the woods and climbed up the hill.

"Let's stop and eat," Stumpy said when they reached a mossy clearing. "I'm hungry. My arms hurt."

"Mine too," Joey agreed. "And my legs ache. I've never pulled that far before."

The boys looked around furtively to make sure they were safe. Then they sat down on a dry outcropping and dug into the pillowcase. Heavy dew moistened the moss and grasses so they kept the sheets and pillowcase tucked on their laps. Each boy ripped off a hunk of bread and chewed quietly.

Joey felt an uneasy mixture of fear and exhilaration. He wanted to throw his hands up and shout at the top of his lungs I'm *free!* He wanted to flop back in the damp clearing and roll over and over in the moss and Easter lilies and shooting stars. He wanted to pick handfuls of the flowers and throw them up into the air in victory. But he had to be cautious. Someone might hear.

"We are outta there, Stumpy. Gone. It's the open tracks for us now."

"We're gonna make it, Joey," Stumpy agreed, then he groaned as he stretched his arms and shoulders.

The sun, already up over the hills, had burned off the clouds and now filtered through the tall trees. It felt warm on the boys' tired bodies.

"Let's go," Stumpy said as he stuffed one last bite of bread in his mouth.

"I'm ready." Joey put the remaining food back into the

pillowcase then threw it over his shoulder as he stood up. Stumpy wrapped the sheets around his neck and headed up the hill. In only a few dozen steps they reached the train tracks. They could hear a loud clanging and buzzing from the sawmill so they cut across the tracks and headed up into the woods on the other side. Once they were safely past the mill they ran back down the hill and into the clearing. Soon the boys were running tirelessly along the tracks. Their legs were light and the wind whipped freely through their hair. When they heard a train forging up behind them, they ran into the trees until it passed. Joey was tempted to jump onto one of the open cars, but the train was going too fast.

The sun was high above their heads before the boys slowed down. Stumpy walked a few paces behind Joey. Soon they were both scuffing their feet.

"I sure hope I get to see Gramps when I get home," Stumpy said as he caught up to Joey. "I got another letter from Lucas. He said he thought Gramps was still in the hospital. Last he heard he wasn't doing so good."

In all the excitement of escaping, Joey had completely forgotten about Stumpy's grandpa.

"I told him I would come right back and look after him. That was a long time ago, Joey. Wonder if he thinks I forgot."

"He'd never think that. He knows you're on your way. Dad says that old people know stuff without you telling them," Joey tried to reassure him. "You're gonna be there soon."

The boys began to notice clearings in the woods along the tracks. They could see fields ahead dotted with barns and houses, and the train tracks ran right through the open country.

"I think we better rest here," Joey said. "Then we better not follow the tracks for a while. We gotta stick to the woods."

"Yeh, but what if we get lost?" Stumpy asked.

"We must be heading into Duncan. We just gotta keep our eyes on the tracks until we get past the town," Joey explained.

He looked ahead. Looming over the tracks was a mountain that looked like the profile of a man's face.

"Hey, I got an idea. See that mountain, Stumpy? Don't forget what it looks like. It looks like a man's nose and then his lips and his big bony chin. If we keep it straight ahead we'll know we're going in the right direction. We can get back to the tracks once we're past the town."

The boys ran along the edge of the woods and skirted the town, avoiding any danger of being caught. Then they climbed a long hill and rejoined the train tracks at the top.

"Time to rest," Joey said.

"What time do you think it is?"

Joey looked at the sun sitting low in the western sky above the mountains. "Probably four or five."

"I didn't know how tired I was." Stumpy lay flat out on his back.

"Me neither. We walked all day."

"Imagine what they are saying at Kuper right now."

"No kidding." Joey grinned. "Brother Jerry will be fuming. Can't you see Father Maynard? His face will be all red. He'll be flapping his hands."

"We made it, Joey. We made it."

"I wonder what Telf told them. Do you think they went to your Auntie Martha's place?"

"Probably. Wonder what she said."

The boys ripped off large hunks of bread and chewed slowly. Although they hadn't eaten since morning, they were more tired than hungry.

They lay back for a few minutes and soaked in the warm late-afternoon sun. A slight breeze rustled through the new growth of the oaks and maples interspersed amongst the tall firs.

"We better not sit around too long or I won't be able to get up," Stumpy groaned.

"I feel like falling asleep." Joey pulled out the rest of the cookies and tossed a couple to Stumpy. "Here, these will make you feel better."

They munched happily, satisfied they were safe. So far they had successfully dodged the trains, they hadn't seen one wild animal, other than a few deer grazing in the grassy meadows, and they hadn't got caught.

"Here." Joey passed Stumpy two carrots.

"Can you believe we really did it?" Joey said as he stood up and tucked the rest of the food back in the pillowcase—barely half a loaf of bread and four apples. He hoped they wouldn't get too hungry tomorrow.

Stumpy got up reluctantly and stretched.

"Back to the tracks," he said.

The hills of the Malahat appeared higher as the sun sank down in the west. The boys were walking slower now and saying less. When they heard the evening train coming toward them, they jumped into the broom that was now clustered on both sides of the tracks. They sat and watched the passengers who were staring out the window as the train passed. Joey was sure a woman with a large brown hat saw him. She seemed to look him right in the eye.

"Do you think anyone saw us, Stumpy?" he asked anxiously.

"I doubt it."

"That was a close call. Those passengers were looking right at us." Joey could see the look on the lady's face in his mind's eye. It was unsettling.

"How about we tuck in for the night?" he asked a little farther down the track. "Let's hit the hills and get some sleep."

"Okay with me." Stumpy was tired. Anything other than

walking another step was fine with him.

They waded their way through the thick broom and scampered up the bluff cut into the hill. The woods were thick with undergrowth. They clomped through bracken fern until they reached a mossy outcropping.

"Looks soft enough for me." Joey dropped the pillowcase.

Stumpy handed Joey one sheet and unrumpled the other. The lush, deep moss billowed under the boys as they lay down. Each boy wrapped himself in a sheet and tumbled onto the soft bed. They shivered in the evening chill.

"Did it have to get cold so fast once the sun went down?" Stumpy's teeth chattered. He rolled as close to Joey as he could get. Pretty soon the boys could feel each other's heat.

Joey lay on his back and gazed into the clear, deep blue night sky. Millions of stars brightened the woods. There wasn't a cloud to be seen. It was still now, but the woods were not quiet. He could hear something. It sounded like an animal looking for a place to sleep. Maybe it was a deer. Or maybe a bear, a cougar or a raccoon. He thought he could hear bats flying from one tree to the next and maybe an owl calling in the distance. He wasn't sure. He had never slept in the hills before. But surprisingly the sounds didn't scare him. He felt safe with the animals. He hoped they knew that.

Stumpy lay perfectly still. "Do you think there are any bears or cougars up here in the bush?"

"Yeh, probably."

"Do you think we are safe?"

"Yeh."

Joey felt Stumpy relax as his breathing slowed. Then he heard a snort. Stumpy was asleep.

6

THE NEXT THING JOEY KNEW, THE SUN WAS SHINING IN HIS face and he heard the woods—alive. He looked up. A robin, perched on a low branch just above them, was singing a beautiful morning song. Above, a woodpecker was busy drilling holes. Joey lay still for a few minutes, listening to the sounds of the woods. It was like music.

"Hey, Stumpy. Morning."

Stumpy tried to straighten his legs, but he had wrapped himself and his sheet into a big knot.

"Wow, Joey. I'm stiff and I'm starving and how am I gonna get out of this thing." Stumpy wrestled with his sheet to try to break free.

The boys sat up and spread the rest of the food on the pillowcase. Half a loaf of bread and four apples. They both looked at the miserable little meal and then at each other.

"I'm starving. This just ain't gonna do it." Stumpy shook his head. "This isn't even breakfast." He broke the bread evenly into two pieces.

Once they finished the bread they each munched on an apple and then each put an apple in his pocket. Stumpy stuffed the sheets into the pillowcase.

"Sure hope we're close," Stumpy said as he stood up.

It was warm and the boys ran most of the morning once they worked out the cramps from the night before. The tracks cut high into the hills. Sometimes the boys could see for long distances over the thickly forested mountain range. Sometimes the trees loomed overhead so they could hardly see ahead at all.

Joey saw a clearing down the tracks and ran ahead to see what it was. Suddenly he stopped. "Gawd, Stumpy. Look at this!"

Stumpy caught up and then stopped next to Joey.

"Holy! The mountain has been cut in half."

The boys backed up and held on to each other as they stretched their necks to look down into the giant ravine.

At the bottom, a rushing river cut its way through the sharp rocks. The only thing joining the mountain together was a narrow wooden trestle.

Joey eyed the elaborate webbing, which climbed up the gigantic ravine and held the tracks in place.

Stumpy stared. "We gotta cross that thing?" His eyes didn't blink.

"You see any other way of getting to the other side?" Joey asked.

The boys looked down the steep sides of the crevice. There was no doubt about it—they had only one choice. Joey went first. He stepped gingerly toward the trestle. Stumpy hung back for a few moments and then followed.

Joey's knees felt like jelly. The wrenching in his stomach felt like more fear than anything he had ever experienced. Maybe terror. After a few tentative steps, he crouched down and crawled forward on his hands and wobbly knees. He kept his eyes trained on the thick fir planks ahead. He made sure he didn't look down or up or to one side or the other. And he tried not to think about what would happen if a train came along.

And Joey didn't look back to see what Stumpy was doing. For now, he forgot completely about his friend.

Once he reached the other side he made sure to keep crawling until he was sure he was safe. Then he rolled onto his bottom and massaged his aching knees. Stumpy caught up and collapsed beside him.

Stumpy began to laugh. "You should have seen your butt creeping across that thing!"

"And what about yours?" Joey laughed too. "We must have

looked pretty funny on our hands and knees."

Once their knees recovered, the boys got up and ran on, filled with renewed energy and pride.

Hours later they reached a stream. The sun was high above their heads now. They kneeled down and gulped the water, then pulled out their last apples. They bit into them ravenously.

"How far we got?" Stumpy asked. "What do you think? I'm pretty tired."

"Don't know," Joey replied. "I don't know where we are. Victoria's got to be up ahead. Pretty close now." At least he hoped so.

"Wonder if we're lost. Wonder if the railway tracks don't go to Victoria. Wonder if we should have followed the road instead."

"You better quit wondering, Stumpy, 'cause it's kinda late now. The tracks will bring us somewhere, and I'm still thinking it's Victoria."

The boys got started again. The rest and the long drink had refreshed them, but they weren't running anymore.

Stumpy was losing confidence. "What are we going to do if we get to Victoria? How are we going to get home?"

"I know people in Victoria. We can wait around the streets until we see someone we know. I got relatives who live there. We'll find someone who knows our family. We can do it, Stumpy. We got this far." Joey didn't want to think too hard about it. All he knew was that it had to work out one way or another.

The boys trudged on. Eventually the sun sank low in the sky. Joey peered ahead into the glare. "Hey, look. There's a sign."

The boys ran up and stared at the big brown sign with gold letters: E-S-Q-U-I-M-A-L-T.

"Well, look at that!" said Joey excitedly. "Esquimalt! It says Esquimalt! That's right next to Victoria. That's where my auntie and uncle live. And they live right beside the railway tracks. I know it. Once, we visited their place and the trains went right past the door. We're there, Stumpy. We made it. Uncle Willie and Auntie Phyllis. They'll get us home."

Joey felt as light as air as he ran past the sign. All his aches and pains, his cramps and worries disappeared. He couldn't wait to see his relatives.

He threw his arms into the air and danced down the tracks, shouting wildly, "We did it! We escaped! We're free, really free."

He slowed down when he saw the station ahead. A few people were milling around on the platform. Joey tucked the pillowcase and sheet under his arm and straightened out his hair.

"Stumpy. Fix your hair and tuck in your shirt."

The two boys walked through the station. No one looked at them with suspicion or said a thing. No one seemed to care at all. Two scruffy Indian kids walking through a train station—nothing wrong with that, Joey thought.

Uncle Willie's place wasn't far from the station.

"There it is, Stumpy! Uncle Willie's." The boys took off like a shot right to the front door.

Joey knocked and Auntie Phyllis opened the door. "Good Lord, Willie!" She turned and left the boys standing on the porch. "You will never believe what landed on our doorstep. Joey, my boy, what on earth are you doing here?"

Auntie Phyllis clapped her hands together. She mussed Joey's hair and pinched and kissed his cheeks as she let them in.

"This is a surprise today. Good Lordy, my boy. Oh and mind my bad manners. Who have you brought with you?" she asked.

"This is Stumpy, Auntie."

"And where are you from, Stumpy? Who's your momma and daddy?"

"I'm from Pauquachin. My grandpa is Abel Dennis," Stumpy replied.

"Oh, I was sorry to hear about Abel, Stumpy. Fine man and respected elder," Auntie Phyllis said, suddenly quiet.

Joey looked over at Stumpy. The boy's head dropped to his chest.

Then Stumpy looked up at Auntie Phyllis. "I came home to look after him. He was in the hospital," Stumpy added. "Is he all right?"

Joey could see that Stumpy didn't understand.

"Oh, dear Lord." Auntie reached out and held Stumpy's shoulders. "I shouldn't be the one to tell you, son. Haven't you spoken to your family yet?"

"No," Stumpy said. "I've been at school. They don't tell us nothing out there."

"Well, then, I just gotta tell you. You see they put your grandpa in the hospital a few months back. And they say that hospital didn't do a good thing for him—he never made it, sonny. They buried him a couple of weeks ago."

Stumpy buried his head in Auntie's chest and held her tight. Joey's heart sank. All the escaping and excitement . . . and now? Nobody at home for Stumpy? His grandpa—dead?

Auntie rubbed Stumpy's head a little and then turned to Joey. "Don't tell me you've run away all the way from Kuper Island." She pulled her glasses off, then curled her eyebrow and gave Joey one of those I-can't-believe-my-eyes-and-ears looks.

"Willie!" Auntie called out. "Willie, get in here. Your nephew Joey and Abel Dennis' grandson have run away from Kuper. We've got them right here in the kitchen!"

As soon as she said "kitchen" Joey realized he could smell deer stew. Auntie Phyllis took them by the shoulders and marched them over to the table. Then she pushed them into chairs, grabbed a couple of bowls, spooned out the stew and plopped some in front of each boy.

"Here, eat up." Auntie rummaged in her shelves and pulled out some sliced bread.

Uncle Willie entered the room. "Good golly, Phyl. What did the cat drag in?" He stepped up behind his nephew and cuffed him affectionately on the back of his head.

"How'd you guys ever make it here?" he asked.

Joey told the whole story.

"Well, Joseph Jones," he said, standing back to take a close look, "I'm proud of you. You are made of tough stuff. But I'm afraid you got more trouble ahead of you than behind you. You know your mother is afraid of those school people. You'll have a lot of talking to do if you're going to convince her to let you stay home."

Then he turned to Stumpy. "Welcome to our place, young man. I'm real sorry about your grandpa. We had a lot of respect for him in these parts. He was a good man."

Joey hadn't thought about what would happen when he got home. What if Mom and Dad sent him back to Kuper? What about Stumpy, especially now that his grandpa was dead?

"Luck's on our side," Uncle Willie continued. "We are taking a trip out to Tsartlip tomorrow afternoon. Edgar Jimmy's giving us a ride and you kids can jump on. And I'll bet Edgar'll drive the boy to Pauquachin."

The warm stew felt good. Neither boy had eaten food this good since they left home. Joey wiped the last drops of gravy from his bowl with a slice of bread.

Auntie Phyllis looked pleased. Then her smile disappeared.

"Looking at the two of you makes me think about that place all over again. You know, I was eight years old when I went to Kuper. It was only three days after we buried my dad." ·

She sighed. "When they came for me, Mom grabbed so tight on my shoulder. She tucked my little doll Eliza under my arm as I left and kissed my forehead. I turned around and saw her long, brown skirt and bright red shawl go through the door.

"I didn't see Mom after that. Oh, the remembering brings it all back. My first Christmas at the school was the worst. They said Mom was sick, so I couldn't go home. I watched all the other children get onto the boat. Only three girls stayed behind. It was right after Christmas, one of the nuns told me that Mom had died. She said Mom got sick once I left and never got better. I think she died of a broken heart. First Dad left her then me.

"After that, Kuper was my home. I stayed there until I was fifteen. That's when they told me I was too old to be there anymore. So I packed my bags and they sent me home. I came back here and stayed with Uncle Fred until he passed away. That's when I met you, Willie."

"That's how you got there and how you got home?" asked Joey.

"That's it."

"Really?" added Stumpy. "What was it like when you were at Kuper?"

Auntie Phyllis shrugged. "Well," she said slowly, "I remember I kept Eliza under my pillow all the time. At night I told her everything. She was my best friend. When I was about ten, she was getting all scruffy and frayed. I tried to keep her clean and neat 'cause I was always afraid the nuns would throw her out.

"Then one night I headed to my bed and, as usual, lifted my pillow to get Eliza. She wasn't there. I looked all over the room. I checked my cubbyhole, under the bed. Then I started to panic. I ran around the room, lifting everyone's pillows. Sister Donna Marie saw what was going on and came over to me.

"'Phyllis,' she said. She looked really mad. 'What are you looking for?'

"'Eliza,' I said. I was almost crying by then. 'Where's Eliza?'

"'Don't you think you are too old for Eliza now? And anyway, the doll is old and dirty.'

"By this time, I was bawling. 'But Eliza's my best friend,' I told her. But she just walked away with a disgusted look on her face. She didn't tell me what they did to my doll or anything. I cried every night for weeks."

Uncle Willie reached out and patted Auntie Phyllis' hand.

She shook her head and chuckled. "Oh, well. That was a long time ago. Willie, do you remember Kuper?"

"I try to forget." Uncle Willie looked serious. "No, not really. It was pretty good out there, I guess. At least it was for me."

He stopped.

Joey gave his uncle a nudge. "C'mon, Uncle, tell us."

"Learning English was pretty hard in our day," he started slowly. "The kids have it easy now. Everybody speaks it at home. Not when we were kids. None of the old people spoke English to us. When I got to Kuper, I was only five and I didn't have a clue what was going on. The first day at class I had to go pee. I figured if I could make a run for the door, I could find the outhouse. So that's what I did. But the brother blocked me off at the door and tossed me back into my desk.

"Then I really had to go. I was crossing my legs and everything. Finally I stood up and shouted out 'I gotta go pee.' I was as polite as I could be, of course. The trouble was I was speaking SENCOTEN. That brother just glared down at me and I just started peeing all over the floor.

"Gawd, I'll never forget that day standing there in a big puddle of pee. I don't know what the brother was saying, but he waved his hands around and got all red in the face. I didn't get no supper that night. I remember that."

Uncle Willie continued, "I didn't bring nothing from home. Not like your Auntie Phyllis. There weren't toys in those days. Not that I remember. Except when I was five, or six maybe, I watched the older boys fold paper airplanes. I was impressed. I remember going up to the dorm with paper and ripping it, folding it, trying everything to get it to fly. Finally I got a design that really worked. It looked more like a helicopter than a plane, but I stood on the bed and threw it up into the air and it whirled and spun through the air.

"Those paper 'copters kept me busy for days. One day I was up in the dorm, it was really sunny, late in the afternoon. The windows were open and a breeze was coming in. I figured out how to catch the air current. I got up on the windowsill and spun my toy into the breeze. The current picked it up. The thing spun around and around and then flew out the window. It seemed like it sailed forever. I didn't take my eyes off it until it rested a good hundred yards from the building."

Stumpy rested his elbows on the table. "So did you learn anything at Kuper?"

Auntie Phyllis laughed out loud. "I learned to wrap the blankets tight on those mattresses."

Stumpy looked confused. It sounded like nothing had changed.

"There wasn't a wrinkle on our beds. We had to make them

so neat it looked like no one ever slept in them. I learned to weed the garden, scrub the clothes, wash the dishes and pray. There were prayers before breakfast, after breakfast, before lunch, after lunch, before supper, after supper. . . ." Auntie Phyllis' voice trailed away. She looked over at Willie.

"I guess I gotta confess I didn't learn much book stuff out there either," Uncle Willie said. "But I sure learned a lot of other stuff. I learned how to pray, that's for sure. I didn't like it much, though. And once I got out of there I forgot it as quick as I could. They taught us to pray for forgiveness for being Indian. Do you remember that, Phyl?"

He didn't wait for Auntie Phyllis to answer. Uncle Willie's face clouded over.

"Imagine that. They taught us to pray to God and ask him to get rid of the Indian devils inside us. I used to stand there as the brother recited those prayers and I said my own little prayer. 'Thanks for the food and thanks for the place and the sooner God you get me out of here the better.'

"I shouldn't be talking like this to you boys. I didn't have such a bad time out there. I really did learn some stuff and I'm happy for that. They worked us hard. We learned how to be men real early.

"When I was nine or ten, the boys worked from morning till night. We hardly ever sat in class. We built all the fences around the place. We milled the timbers, dug the holes, nailed them up and painted them white.

"Oh, I stood back in the garden with my hands in my pockets and looked that fence up and down. I was one proud boy. It was the most beautiful fence I had ever seen in my life . . . and I can still build one darn good fence.

"By the time I was thirteen or fourteen, they put me on as foreman when we built the chicken sheds. Ernie, Alex, Elmer, Johnston and me. That was the crew, and I was the head man.

Those were the best chicken sheds you are ever gonna come across. I bet the chickens are still happy laying eggs out there."

Joey and Stumpy hung on every word. Uncle Willie was beginning to enjoy his storytelling. "They had me feeding the pigs. That was my regular job. Every morning it was up and out of bed and straight out to the pig barn by five o'clock. In the winter it was pretty black out there. I remember heading out there in the dark, freezing my butt off.

"The trouble with feeding the pigs on those dark mornings was that, once I got out to the barn, I had to find my way inside the stall door and clear around the corner to find the darn light switch.

"One morning, it was as cold a January or February morning as I've ever known— and I was sleepy. I staggered outside, shivering to beat heck. I stumbled across the crusty grass to the slop house to get the feed. I filled up two buckets, right to the brim. They weighed as much as me if you put them together. I dragged that slop clear across the yard to the pig shed. It was so dark outside, I never could've found it if it weren't for my nose. That place stunk. When I got there I scrambled around, looking for the door handle.

"Once I got in, I set one bucket down and then reached around looking for the light switch. You'd have laughed if you had seen me that morning. My hands were frozen and I couldn't find the switch. Then no sooner did I find it and turn the light on than I slipped on the icy floor—both feet straight up and then straight down on my butt. Well, that slop bucket went up into the air, turned over and landed right on top of my head.

"There I was. Sitting in it and wearing it at the same time. You should've seen the pigs. They started grunting and squealing as if the whole show was just for them.

"I'll never forget that day. Frozen solid, I picked up the

slop—potato peelings, tea leaves, apple cores—with my bare hands. Then I tossed it to the pigs. And the worst thing was I was flat-out sitting in pig crap. It's a good thing no one was there to watch that mess."

Joey was laughing so hard, he had both hands wrapped around his stomach.

"Gawd, Uncle Willie. I bet you smelled like a pig for days."

Uncle Willie smiled. "Yeh, I sure did. They worked us hard out there. Especially the boys."

"Not especially the boys," Auntie Phyllis protested. "They worked the girls just as hard."

"I guess work was the main thing out there in our day. You remember those clean polished floors, Phyl? That was another job of mine and I was darn proud of it.

"Brother Harland made sure those floors were shining. The senior boys washed and waxed and then the brother got me and James. Yeh, that guy from up Nanoose way. It was me and him. Old Harland got a big chunk of railway tie and wrapped it in a towel. The thing was so big, I could barely hold on to it. We each got one. We got on our hands and knees and shone that sucker of a floor till we could see our faces shining right back at us.

"Sixteen stairs and then the landing. Sixteen more stairs to the second floor. I remember counting them off as we polished. When we finished the stairs we'd sit at the top like we had climbed Mount Everest. It sure felt like it.

"One thing I'm thinking is when they worked us so hard they should have fed us more. Sometimes I was starving. Especially when I got older. We'd get our three squares a day, but after working in the field or building the barns we could have used more food. It got pretty serious over there."

"You could have had half of mine," Auntie Phyllis said,

shaking her head. "The food all tasted the same. Most meals I left on my plate and then afterwards I scooped the whole mess into the garbage can. You better believe it, every day I wished for fried or smoked or dried salmon—or even for a bowl of duck soup."

"I never left a thing on my plate. And if anyone else had any extra I ate that too," Uncle Willie added. "I remember I had one pretty good fight while I was out there, and it was all about food. Peanut butter. Can you believe getting into a fight about peanut butter?

"It was March 13th, 1941. My fourteenth birthday. Mom and Dad were gone by then, and no one else ever remembered my birthday. I never had a birthday present at Kuper. And for some reason every year I thought about it. I didn't expect anything, but I always wished, and that year I was really upset. I wanted something for my birthday. Most kids got packages or cards from home. Some even got money.

"Lenny Taylor's mom always sent him money and he would send for peanut butter when anyone was going over to Chemainus. They'd bring him back a whole tin and he'd hide it in his cubbyhole until night. Then he'd haul it out and eat it after the lights went out. He'd dip his fingers in and scoop a big gob into his mouth. I got pretty disgusted listening to him eat, but I was so jealous some nights I could have killed for his peanut butter.

"Anyway, on my fourteenth birthday I got it in my head that I should get some peanut butter. Well, that morning he'd stashed the tin away but he still smelled like it. You see Lenny was real protective and stingy with his peanut butter. I don't remember anyone getting any. Not even Charlie, his best friend.

"That smell of peanut butter really got me going that morning, it being my birthday and all. I sat on my bed thinking about how it was my birthday. I imagined old Harland coming into the dorm saying 'Hey, Willie. Got mail for you today.' I thought of opening the card. 'Happy birthday, kid. Here's two bucks. Get yourself some peanut butter.' I wished, but I knew I wasn't getting any.

"It never happened, of course. So I sat on my bed until everyone headed off for breakfast. Then I went straight to Lenny's cubbyhole, pulled out the tin of peanut butter and pulled off the lid. Just as I dipped my fingers into the jar Lenny came around the corner looking for his sweater.

"Talk about getting caught with your fingers in the peanut butter! That was me. I didn't even get a chance to taste it. Lenny came at me like a madman.

"'What the hell do you think you are doing?' he was screaming at the top of his lungs.

"The big gob of peanut butter slid off my fingers onto the floor. Then Lenny came flying across the room, stepped in the peanut butter and slid right onto his butt, kicking and screeching. It was a sight. I would've laughed except he got up and started pounding me.

"'You're so poor,' he said, 'you can't even get your own peanut butter.'

"When he said that, I saw red. I went crazy on him. It was the worst fight I had out at Kuper. Not that Lenny was that tough or anything, but I went right out of my mind. I punched and kicked poor Lenny until he was crying. Old Harland got there in time to pull me off and shake me up.

"Lenny was shouting, 'Get off me, you idiot. What's in you? You're crazy!'

"When I stood up and looked at Lenny, he had a bloody nose and a long cut over his eye that was spurting blood everywhere. He was a mess. He was snuffling and sobbing. I couldn't believe it. I wasn't much of a fighter, but I did a lot of damage that morning.

"Everyone stood kinda shocked for a few seconds. Then I said, 'It's my birthday. I'm fourteen and no one even knows I was born. All I want is a tin of peanut butter for my birthday.'

"I started sobbing like a baby and slumped down onto the bed.

"Lenny stopped crying and stared at me. He said, 'Cool down, Willie. Okay, okay, happy birthday!'

"I musta caught Old Harland off guard, 'cause he didn't know what to do. He looked real close at me and said, 'Happy birthday, Willie.' They both left me sitting there. I sat real sombre like and then licked the rest of the peanut butter off my fingers. 'Happy birthday, Willie,' I said to myself.

"I got over my bad feelings pretty quick and the day carried on as usual. Chores, class and nothing for my birthday.

"But just before supper that day, I got the shock of my life. Old Harland meets me in the corridor. He has a big brown paper bag and is holding it with two hands. 'Happy birthday, Willie,' he says.

"That was it. That's all he said. The guy wasn't used to being so sensitive.

"As he walked out the door, I shouted after him, 'Thanks. Thanks for the peanut butter.'

"You know," Uncle Willie said, slapping his hands down on the table, "I still love peanut butter. Best thing in the world!"

"Not as important as a good night's sleep," Auntie Phyllis said firmly, as she stood up. She left the room, then returned with a blanket.

"We've got no space for you boys in the bedroom, but you can sleep on the couch. I'm sure you're tired and it's getting late. Enough about Kuper Island. I'm sure you boys have stories of your own."

The boys followed her to the living room and lay at opposite ends of the couch. They kicked each other's feet

until they were comfortable. Auntie Phyllis covered them
with the blanket.

Soon the warmth from the wood stove sent them into a
deep sleep.

Joey and Stumpy looked out the back window of Edgar
Jimmy's car as it pulled away from the house. The car was
packed. Uncle Willie and Auntie Phyllis sat next to the
boys. Another woman, Joey thought her name was Geraldine,
sat against the other door. Four adults sat in the front. And a
baby.

Joey breathed the stale air from Edgar's cigarette as it filtered over the back seat and eventually permeated the whole
car. His stomach didn't feel so good. His mind went back to
the long-ago car ride to Kuper. . . . He couldn't remember
much except the now-familiar sour feeling of nausea in his
stomach.

When they reached Tsartlip, Edgar stopped the car at the
top of the path. "Gotta let you go here, Joey," he said. "I'll
head right out to Pauquachin and visit Stumpy's family for a
while. I think they're gonna be happy the boy is home from
that school. I heard the last thing old Abel said before he died
was 'Get my grandson home where he belongs.'"

Joey gave Stumpy a quick slap on the back. Stumpy's family were probably going to be more excited to see him than
Joey's mom and dad would be.

"See you, buddy." The boys gave each other a nod.

"We'd better get out here with my nephew," Uncle Willie
said. "My sister Priscilla's gonna need some persuading."

It turned out even Uncle Willie and Auntie Phyllis couldn't
persuade Mom. Not even with Dad on their side.

Mom's afraid, Joey realized, and that's all there is to it.

She held him tight. And he did stay home for a little while.

But in the end, Joey went back to Kuper.

Monica

1

"DUSTY AND MONICA WILL GO WITH SISTER MARY LOUISE."

Father Maynard wheezed with each word, as if something was stuck in his windpipe. Monica watched the beads of sweat form on his forehead and upper lip then drop onto his black gown, which was already stained and damp.

Father Maynard sneered at Dusty. "And, young lady, do you have a *real* name?"

Dusty smiled inside, thankful that Sister Theresa at the Day School had written "Dusty" on the introduction. That way no one at Kuper needed to know she was really Dorothy Jean. "No, sir, I mean, yes, sir. Dusty is my real name."

"And you must be Monica," he said, quickly ignoring Dusty and pointing his pudgy finger at the other girl. His bulging cheeks dimpled into a smile. His small, bird-like eyes looked closely into her face, then slowly dropped down her body.

Monica shivered.

"Welcome to Kuper Island Residential School, Monica. The note here says you are a very bright thirteen-year-old girl—a very good student." His eyes retraced their path back up her body, this time more slowly. "We like good students here at Kuper."

"Now, Sister Mary Louise," he said, at last releasing Monica from his gaze, "make sure you take good care of these girls."

Dusty grabbed Monica's hand and pulled her along behind the sister. Father Maynard didn't appear to notice Dusty's parting glare.

"That man is a pig," she said under her breath. "Did you see how he looked at you?"

Monica was stunned. "Dusty, he makes me sick." How could her father allow this? There had to be some awful mistake.

Sister Mary Louise turned her head and frowned at the girls, almost as if she had heard them. Monica leaned against Dusty, grateful that her friend was holding on. Her knees shook and her head was light.

As they walked along the school corridor, Sister Mary Louise spoke, but her words were like static on the radio. ". . . beds . . . washroom . . . clothes . . . bells . . . " Monica tried, but she could pick up only the odd word here and there. The sister's voice was grating and thick, her accent strange.

It wasn't until Sister Mary Louise said, "Now we go into de teachers' room and cut your hair," that Monica heard her clearly.

"No," Monica blurted, shaken out of her daze. "No. You can't cut my hair."

"Everyone gets hair cut, young lady," she replied in halting English. "And, good clean as well. Take care of de bugs and de dirt."

"No. My hair has never been cut. Never." Monica panicked.

She thought of the promise she had made just before Mom died. "Mom," Monica had said as her mom stroked her long braids, "I will never cut my hair. I will always think of you when I stroke my braids."

Now she held her braids with both hands. "I will tie them up. My hair is clean . . . I have no bugs. Honest, I've never had bugs. My hair is my pride . . . Mom said. Please don't cut it."

Dusty pushed Monica aside and placed herself directly in front of Sister Mary Louise. "You don't understand," Dusty said stubbornly. "Monica can't cut her hair. She promised her mom, who was dying. And now she's dead."

"No, young lady. *You* don't understand. Every new student at Kuper Island Residential School gets hair cut. And something else you don't understand. Don't argue with teachers. When I say get hair cut, you get hair cut."

Sister Mary Louise reached around Dusty, grabbed Monica's arm and pushed her down onto a chair. She picked up a huge pair of shears.

"Please, no. Please, no," Monica begged.

"Monica, stop her!" Dusty shouted. "Get up and run!"

Monica was paralyzed. Dusty lunged toward the scissors just as the sister cut through one of Monica's thick braids.

Dusty slumped back against the table. "You've done it now! Look, you've done it now!" she shouted as tears began to well up in her eyes. "You've cut Monica's hair. And she promised her mom."

Helplessly, Monica watched her thick, shiny, long, black braid flop to the floor. Dead. Seconds later the other braid fell next to it. She sat, powerless, as the sister sawed and hacked her hair from side to side. Prickly spikes scratched her neck and down her chest.

"Mom, I'm so sorry. Mom, I'm so sorry," Monica sobbed.

When she was finished, Sister Mary Louise laid the shears on the table. "All finished," she said. "Now was dat bad? Tink how easy it will be to keep dat mop clean now."

Monica hung her head on her chest—shattered.

"I'm finished with you," the sister snapped. "Now off de chair. It Dusty's turn."

Monica lifted her head and looked at her friend. Pale blotches stained Dusty's face as her lips tightened and her eyes grew dark and sharp. Dusty staggered backwards against the wall, keeping her eye on Sister Mary Louise. Dusty's knuckles whitened as she clenched her fists.

"Oh, no. You aren't getting your hands on my hair. Not a fat chance."

Monica crept around to the far side of the room. The sister charged toward Dusty. Just as she clawed at Dusty's arm, the door opened and Brother Jerry walked in.

"Do you need some help with the new girls, sister?" He grinned, but his eyes were cold.

"Dis one is a fighter." Sister Mary Louise pointed. "Dis one tinks she can talk back. I cut de first one but dis one is going to be de hard one."

Dusty crouched down and dodged back and forth as the two teachers tried to grab her. Finally Brother Jerry caught her arm and forced her onto the chair.

"You animals. Let me go." Dusty squirmed and kicked and flung her head back and forth. But Brother Jerry held her down while Sister Mary Louise picked up the shears and began hacking away at her hair. Soon Dusty gave up the fight and collapsed in a heap in the chair. Tears streamed down her cheeks as thick chunks of black hair dropped to the floor.

Monica huddled in the corner of the room. She felt like she was in the middle of a bad dream. Everything was distant, unreal. Dusty's cries echoed back and forth, while the voices of Sister Mary Louise and Brother Jerry faded in and out, like waves crashing and receding. An eerie feeling overtook her as Father Maynard's voice seemed to murmur in her ear and then disappear. She felt nothing.

The moment passed, and Monica focused again on the sight of Dusty's hair, now shorter than her longest finger, except for the odd bits sticking up.

Then Brother Jerry poured foul-smelling gasoline on the girls' heads while Sister Mary Louise rubbed it into their scalps. "Dat will do de bugs," she said as she wiped her hands on a rag. "Now be in de dining room—supper in ten minutes."

Sister Mary Louise hurriedly pushed the girls out the door.

Dusty lifted her hands to her head. She felt the short spikes of hair prickling against her fingers.

"Oh, no, Monica. Oh, no. No. No. What have they done?" she cried, weeping uncontrollably.

Monica held on to her friend. She had never seen Dusty cry. Usually it was Dusty holding Monica and she wasn't sure what to do. She ran her fingers through Dusty's hair and tried to fix it.

Monica's own head felt strange. She raised her hand to feel her hair, but she stopped, fingers suspended in the air, just above the sharp ends. She wouldn't touch it. She couldn't touch it. Her hand fell limp.

Dusty rubbed her head furiously, as if the hair would return—as if it would grow back instantly.

"We stink, Dusty," Monica said matter-of-factly. "We have ten minutes to wash this stuff out of our hair. Come on."

When they got to the washroom, Monica lowered her head into the sink as Dusty soaped and rinsed her friend's hair. The soap smelled rotten but it was a little better than the gasoline. Monica thought of Mom and her sister Amelia. She thought of Dad and Donnie and the little boys, Reggie and Ronnie. She thought of everything but her hair. Dusty rubbed her head with a towel and brushed her hair in quick, short strokes while Monica's hands caressed her invisible braids.

Then Monica washed and towel-dried Dusty's hair. She tried to brush the short spikes flat, but now that the hair was clean, it stuck up worse than before. When Monica was finished, Dusty looked into the mirror facing the girls.

"Monica!" she wailed. "Monica, look what they've done to me. I look so ugly. I look like a boy." She held her hands tightly over her head as if she could hide her awful haircut.

"Come on, Dusty," Monica said flatly. She moved carefully, making sure the mirror did not reflect her image.

They hurried down the corridor toward the dorm to change for supper. On the way, three girls passed them. Monica looked at each girl's hair—chopped short right off above her ears. Like someone had put a bowl over her head and cut around it. Again, she had that odd feeling of being in a dream. She closed her eyes.

Dad didn't know this would happen. He never would have let them take her if he knew they were going to cut her hair.

"I guess we are numbers now," Dusty said, pulling their newly assigned school clothes out of their cubbyholes. Sister

Mary Louise had marked each piece of clothing with a number. "Call me number fifty-six."

"Call me number eighty-seven," Monica replied.

She slowly unbuttoned her blouse and slipped it off. She shook the hair off the blouse before she carefully folded it and placed it in the laundry bin. Dusty wiped Monica's shoulders and back clean. Then Monica turned and wiped the last traces of Dusty's hair from her back. The girls finished dressing and left the room—and their hair, forever.

"You know, Monica," Dusty said quietly as they walked toward the dining hall, "I am going to hate this place."

"It's going to be all right, Dusty. Our hair will grow back."

"Take a look, Monica," she replied. "Just take a great big look. You don't see one girl here with long hair. Our hair will grow back all right. Then what do you think they will do? What are they going to do, Monica—let your braids grow down to your knees? I doubt it. They'll just cut them again." Dusty raised her voice.

"Just 'cause your dad wants you to go to school, Monica, doesn't mean he knows a thing about what's going on at this place."

Monica nodded. Dusty was right. Dad must have known nothing about the Kuper Island school.

Dusty surveyed the girls lined up in the corridor outside the dining room.

"I don't know why you stay around this place," she said loudly to no one in particular. "I'm sure not sticking around here too long. You look like monkeys with your hair cut like that. That's the last time they are getting scissors near my head. I can tell you that." Dusty made sure the girls heard her.

The girls stared at Dusty and Monica. "That's what you think," one girl said. "They do whatever they want in this place. You'll get used to it."

"Not this girl," Dusty snapped back, pointing at her chest. "This girl will never get used to being pushed around."

Monica quietly fell in line and watched. All the girls looked the same. The same blouses—some were blue, but most were flour-sack beige. The same skirts—the skinny girls had skirts wrapped around twice and the big girls were in skirts that barely covered them. Everyone's hair was chopped off straight above their ears—everyone's except Dusty's. Her hair looked like a boy's crewcut.

That night Monica lay in her bed and reached for her braids. When she felt the emptiness resting on her chest where the braids had been, she clasped her hands together, closed her eyes and thought of her mom.

She fell asleep and dreamed of Mom brushing her hair, over and over. She didn't see her mom's face, but she heard the smooth sound of the brush moving effortlessly through her silky hair. She heard Mom's soft voice. "Monica. You are a beautiful girl. Your hair is a gift. Wear it with pride." Mom divided the hair into equal parts and skillfully twisted it into glossy braids. Monica held the invisible braids in her hands while she slept.

2

ONE WEEK AFTER MONICA ARRIVED AT KUPER SHE RECEIVED a letter.

"Monica," Sister Mary Louise called out after supper. "You have mail."

She handed her an envelope. "Make sure your father seals it better next time. You're lucky you didn't lose it."

Monica looked at the envelope. There was no return

address on the corner. Just the address—Kuper Island Residential School, Kuper Island, BC— neatly printed on the bottom right side. She ran her fingers across the seal. Someone had torn the envelope open and then tried clumsily to reseal it.

"Thank you," she called out to Sister Mary Louise as she walked away down the corridor.

Monica ran to the dorm and jumped onto her bed. Her hands trembled as she pulled the crumpled letter free and flattened it gently on the blanket.

She didn't recognize the writing.

Dear Monica,

I miss you. I hope you are doing well at the school. We all miss you.

I need to apologize to you. My heart is heavy and you must understand that I was wronged and so, my dear, were you. Please understand that I did not know Agent Macdonald was coming on Wednesday to pick you up. It wasn't until Sister Theresa came to call after school that I was informed that you were already taken.

You are my pride and joy. Since the day you were born I have known that you are a special girl. You learned to talk before any other child your age. You remembered everything you were taught. You learned to knit and help in the house while you were almost still a baby. Monica, you have special talent.

One day when you were just four years old, your mother and I were sitting at the kitchen table and you picked up an old newspaper. You said, "What do these words mean, Daddy? I want to read." Monica, we knew you had a special gift. Our people need your gift.

Our people are poor. They are having a hard time learning

the ways of the white people. I can only just write this letter with help. But you are our gift. You will learn to read and write. You will become a teacher and you will come back and help our people. That is why I agreed to send you to Kuper. They will teach you everything.

My daughter I must explain. We had no time to say goodbye. Please believe me. I agreed that you should go to the school, but no one told me when they were taking you. You must not believe that I abandoned you. I am as angry as you must be that they did not tell us when they were coming. They did not give us time to prepare.

Please don't let our lack of goodbyes put anger in your heart. I explained everything to Donnie, Amelia and Ronnie and Reggie. They miss you like I do. Amelia is taking care of things the best way she can. We all miss your mom and love her in our hearts. She is proud of you, Monica, and watching over you. You have her brains and her beauty and you will make her proud.

Your grandfather is still angry with me for letting them take you to the school. He doesn't understand our need to learn English. He wants to make sure you never forget your own SENCOTEN language. Please don't.

Remember where you are from. Concentrate on where you are going. Learn everything you can from those people, Monica, and bring it back home. Agent Macdonald told me the walls of that school are filled with books. Read every one of them. Write us a letter and tell us everything you are learning and what you are doing. We want to know how you are.

Mrs. Mayber kindly helped me with this letter. She says hello.

    We miss you.
    Dad

Monica rolled onto her back and rested the letter over her heart. The sun streamed in through the window. She felt hot. She closed her burning eyes, which were suddenly filled with tears. She covered her face with her pillow and cried uncontrollably.

She ached to hold Amelia and Ronnie and Reggie. She wanted to talk to Donnie. She could see them running up the path from the beach, barefooted and sun roasted. Their little bodies, almost black from the summer sun, would be streaked with dried salt water and speckled with sand. Monica breathed in deeply and smelled sea water and kelp and dried clams.

She squeezed her eyes tight shut so she could see home for one more moment.

Then she sat up and neatly folded the letter and placed it carefully back into the envelope. She stared across the quiet dorm, with its rows of beds tightly wrapped in matching blankets. Then she retreated into the blankness that filled her mind.

A girl sat down on the next bed. Her voice interrupted Monica's trance. "You're lucky," the girl said. "You got a letter from home."

"Yes," Monica said. "I guess I am." She didn't feel lucky.

"My name's Agnes."

"I'm Monica."

"Any news from home?"

"Yeh, my dad explained why they came and took me here to Kuper without telling us."

"They did that to me too, but I never heard from home until Christmas. That was three years ago."

Monica wiped her face on her pillow.

"You'll get used to it here," Agnes said. "We all do. It's not so bad after a while."

3

AFTER THE INITIAL SHOCK OF COMING TO KUPER, MONICA got used to the bells, prayers, lineups, kitchen chores, and laundry. She got used to sewing the students' clothes and darning the socks. Her fingers were so quick and skillful that when she finished her darning, she was given the other girls' work to finish. But she didn't mind too much. It made the time pass.

She remembered her mom's words as she threaded her needle and pulled the darning wool through sock after sock. "My dear, a woman with quick hands is a treasure to her husband and children." Monica thought of the long winter nights by the coal oil lamp, sitting next to her mother. Mom's knitting needles clicked rapidly, making a pleasant song in Monica's ears. Sometimes Monica would look up, and Mom's eyes would be closed while the beautiful designs emerged on her sweater.

Monica enjoyed the handwork at Kuper, but the shelves weren't full of books like Agent Macdonald had promised Dad. She asked around to find books to read. Sister Mary Louise found her old copies of *Little Women* and *Anne of Green Gables*. And when Brother Eubieus heard she liked to read so much, he gave her two books he had brought from home.

When she finished her school work she curled up on her bed with Meg, Jo, Beth and Amy.

Class work was easy. It didn't take much for Monica to get As on every assignment she handed in. She soon realized that the teacher didn't expect much from the students. Sometimes her writing was messy and still she would get an A. Sister Mary Louise was more strict about how they cleaned the floors than how they did their school work.

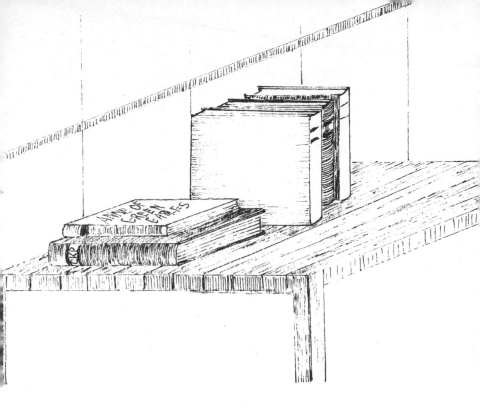

One day, while Monica and Agnes kneeled on the floor, cleaning as usual, the sister met them in the corridor. "You girls make sure not one speck dust left on dat floor. When you finish de corridor you mop de dorm." She bent down and examined the glassy wood floor.

"Look dere! You blind?" Sister Mary Louise pointed to a little dustball clinging to the baseboard.

Monica obediently picked up the dust and placed it in the garbage bag.

"Someday you be somebody's wife. You be good wife. You know dey say, 'Cleanliness beside godliness.'" Sister Mary Louise turned around and walked away.

"Cleanliness beside godliness. Someday I be somebody's wife," Agnes mimicked. "Clean, clean, clean, Monica."

Monica stopped and surveyed the long, polished floor. "I knew how to mop and sweep and polish before I came to this place," she said sullenly. "I came here to learn so I can be a teacher."

"Where are you from, Monica? Have you lost your mind?" Agnes looked at her in shock. "Indian girls aren't teachers. Hasn't anyone ever told you that? Indian girls learn to mop the floor and cook potatoes. Clean, cook, and when you are finished cleaning, then clean some more."

"That's what some people say, but that's not what Dad says. And that's not what Mom said before she died. She said that Indian girls can do whatever any other girls do. And Dad says that I can become a teacher."

Agnes studied Monica's face carefully. "You mean it, don't you, Monica? You are really serious about that teaching stuff."

"I mean it. You could learn more than how to clean floors too, Agnes."

"I can't read books all the time."

"Read *and* write. I'm gonna make it and you can too, Agnes. One day you'll hear that Monica Sam is a teacher."

Just then, Monica heard a door open. It was Father Maynard's office. She grabbed Agnes' arm and pulled her down the hall toward the staircase.

"Monica, could you come here for a moment?"

She pretended not to hear him and turned for the stairs. Monica always made sure she avoided the priest.

"Monica," he called louder. "I have a favour to ask of you."

Her heart sank. She held her breath as she walked back up the corridor and stood in front of him.

"Yes, Father Maynard. What would you like?"

"Now that's a good girl. That's what I like to hear." Monica couldn't hold her breath any longer. She breathed in, smelling stale perspiration and musty onions.

The priest rested his sweaty hand on Monica's shoulder. Then he began to rub her neck.

"You do such a good job mopping the corridor. I want you to clean up my office too." He pressed her into his office and closed the door.

When the bell rang for afternoon class, Monica darted back down the hall.

Agnes was waiting for her outside the classroom. "What happened to you?" she said.

"When the bell rang, I told him I couldn't be late for class." Monica felt a little dizzy.

Agnes looked confused. "No, I mean, before. What happened before that?"

"What do you mean? There was no before. I ran out of his room as fast as I could." Monica's voice quavered and her heart pounded violently in her chest.

"Please," she begged, grabbing onto Agnes' sleeve, "don't leave me alone with him in his room. I don't want him near me. I don't want him calling me that name, like I am his pet."

Agnes looked into her friend's desperate face and tried to smile. "I'll try, Monica." She shuddered. "He is so disgusting."

Monica slumped into her desk. She rubbed the palms of her hands into her eyes to black out the feelings. She reached for her braids, but instead, she clasped her hands together when they met in the empty space in front of her.

She looked over at Agnes. She was thankful to have a friend now that Dusty wasn't around much. Something had changed with Dusty. It was the haircut. She hadn't been the same since that day. Now she had found new friends—girls Monica avoided as much as possible.

Monica glanced over her shoulder to the back of the classroom. Nellie and Vivian sat next to Dusty. They were whispering back and forth and laughing together. They were a threesome, best left alone. She knew the other girls kept their distance from the three as well, partly from fear and partly because they could never tell what Dusty and her friends would say or do next.

One night, just after Thanksgiving, Dusty came over to Monica's bed as she was changing into her nightgown.

"Monica," Dusty said, "when are you gonna admit your dad is wrong? You walk around with those stupid books in your hand. Do you really think this place will teach you anything?"

Dusty pinned her against the bed. "Come on, Monica." Dusty's voice was loud and taunting. "Tell us. What are you learning here? Will your daddy be happy with all the good stuff they're teaching you?"

Monica couldn't speak. Why was Dusty doing this?

"Y'know what, Monica? Your daddy's wrong. You ain't never gonna be a teacher, and you know it."

Monica's heart pounded violently. No. Her dad had to be right. It's why she was here.

Dusty smiled nastily. "You know what you're gonna learn here Monica? I mean apart from cooking and sewing and cleaning? Wanna know what else you're gonna learn?"

Dusty stopped and scowled. "Well, one thing you're gonna learn is that Indians gotta stick up for ourselves, and whites got a few things to learn."

Monica nodded, hoping that Dusty would stop, that she would leave her alone. "I guess so."

But Dusty wasn't finished. She towered over the bed so Monica couldn't stand up. "I'm right, LP. I'm right, LP. And you know it," Dusty taunted.

"Stop it, Dusty! That's mean," Monica cried out.

Please stop it. Please stop it, Monica repeated to herself. She curled up on her bed and covered up with her blanket. Her bones vibrated, and a hot flush crept up behind her ears. Not this again, she thought. Please, Dusty. Stop it.

Soon Nellie and Vivian joined Dusty.

"What's wrong, LP? Don't you like being called LP?" Dusty kept it up. Vivian and Nellie laughed as they tugged at the blanket.

"My name's not LP," Monica whimpered. "My name is Monica. Stop it. Please stop."

She clenched her fists around the blanket and covered her eyes to shut out what was coming next. Her inside voice shouted, *Monica, don't look at them, don't listen to them. It's not true what they are going to say.* But the girls were too loud. She could still hear them.

"Father Maynard's little LP. Hey, come on, Monica, tell us what LP stands for." First one, then another teased and shouted insults.

Soon Monica could hear some of the other girls join in the laughter. If she could just disappear, it would all go away. She reached for her braids. But, once again, her hands reached in the now-familiar emptiness where her braids once hung. She wrung her hands together and tried to think of Mom. There was nothing. Her mind was blank.

Then she heard Sister Mary Louise through the emptiness.

"Stop, you girls!" she shrieked. Monica pulled the blankets down and peered out into the room.

The sister began pulling Dusty, Nellie and Vivian away from Monica's bed.

"Leave her alone," Sister Mary Louise shouted. "Get to bed. All you."

She shoved the girls toward their beds and went back to

Monica. Then she peered down with a strange smirk on her face.

"All right, Monica. Tell us what LP stands for. We would like to hear," she said, her voice mean.

Monica heard the sister's words, but her mind couldn't concentrate.

"Monica," Sister Mary Louise repeated. "Tell us what LP stands for."

"Monica. It stands for Monica."

The sister clasped her hands over her gaping mouth and threw her head back, laughing hysterically.

Monica yanked her nightie over her knees and wrapped it tightly around her legs. Then she pulled the blankets back up over her face.

"LP! LP! LP!" She heard a chorus of voices from the girls in the room.

In the darkness, under her blankets and through the buzz of all the commotion, Monica's mind flashed back to when it all started—the day Sister Mary Louise cut her hair. She had forgotten. But now she remembered Father Maynard had walked into the teachers' room before Brother Jerry and Sister Mary Louise had finished with Dusty. That's right, he was there.

While they'd been hacking Dusty's hair, Father Maynard walked in and picked up one of her braids. He had stroked it slowly, then moved close to her. He'd whispered in her ear. The words were clear for the first time. Monica gagged. She wished she didn't remember.

"You look like a princess. A little princess." His wet lips had moved sloppily as he eyed her body. He'd reached out as if to touch Monica's hair, but instead, rubbed his hand across her breasts. "You are my LP." Then he left the room before the haircut was finished.

Memories flashed into Monica's mind. She thought of the day that she tried to slip past him in the corridor.

"LP," he called to her. "LP, you don't need to be afraid of me. It's our secret. You are my little princess."

He'd pulled Monica close to him. His body had been damp and musty. His breath had smelled like stale smoke and bacon and peanut butter. His voice had rumbled between the snorting in his nostrils and what sounded like a clog in his throat.

"You are a special girl," he'd said as he rubbed himself up against her. "Your dad asked me to take special care of you. Your teachers tell me you are a smart one. Now, LP, if you want extra books to read you must take special care of me, too." He rubbed his sticky fingers up and down her cheeks.

Monica had crossed her legs to keep from wetting herself. She'd gagged back the vomit welling up in her throat.

"Remember, LP. We can take special care of each other," he had called back as he waddled down the hall. Monica had swayed unsteadily as she tried to walk away.

Vivian, Nellie and Dusty had entered the corridor just in time to hear the father.

"You take special care of him, LP," Nellie had hollered. "LP, LP, LP's gonna take special care of fat Maynard."

Now Monica tried to keep her mind from remembering all the times. *Just forget about it,* she yelled to herself. But she couldn't. Everyone knew. And now everyone was laughing and waiting for her to tell the story.

She pulled the blankets away from her face. She knew she couldn't escape.

Sister Mary Louise waited with her hands on her hips. "We're waiting, LP."

"It means little princess," Monica whispered, then turned and covered herself again.

The laughter faded into the distance. She lay still and listened to her ears ring and her heart beat. Monica's body lay in bed while her mind disappeared. Soon she couldn't hear a thing.

Monica lay perfectly still for hours—awake but not there. Finally she opened her eyes and looked around the room. The lights were out. Moonlight cast long, distorted columns of shadow on the wall—like totem poles evenly spaced across the room. It was so bright she could see dust particles dancing in the air. She heard the other sleepers breathing heavily. Someone by the door snored and snorted so loudly that she wondered why the other girls didn't wake up.

The stillness was disturbed by a shuffle in the darkness. Someone had gotten out of bed and was walking toward her. She strained her eyes in fear, wondering who it was and what they wanted.

As the figure got closer, Monica recognized Vivian. She held her sweater tightly over her shoulders and stopped next to Monica's bed.

"Monica," the older girl whispered, so low that Monica could barely hear her. "I want to talk to you."

Vivian sat down beside her. She rested her hand on Monica's shoulder and leaned close to her face.

"Hey, are you awake?" Monica had never heard Vivian sound so kind. "Listen to me. You have to be careful of Maynard. I should know. He used to call me pretty girl. He used to tell me that I could have anything I wanted. But I had to do what he said. Monica, you know what he wants from you, don't you?"

Monica was frozen.

"Monica, you have to believe me. I'm not here to hurt you. I can help." Vivian gently rubbed Monica's back.

Once again all the memories of Father Maynard . . . she'd

hidden them . . . they were rushing back . . . out of their hiding places.

"Vivian," Monica sobbed. "He's already got it."

She reached out and grabbed Vivian's arm. "He takes me into his bedroom and gets whatever he wants. Sister Mary Louise comes to my bed at night, sometimes, and wakes me up. She says that Father Maynard wants to see his little princess. Vivian, he hurts me. I hate him, Vivian. And I hate Sister Mary Louise. She waits around until he's finished. And then she swears at me and tells me I'm dirty. Vivian. What can I do?"

She cried uncontrollably. Vivian bent down and wrapped her arms around Monica. Both girls sobbed.

"I am so sorry, Monica. I am so sorry it's happening to you." Vivian held on. "He will stop. He stopped bugging me when a new girl came from Nanaimo. Some other girl will come to the school and he won't want you anymore. Then she will be his special girl."

"No, Vivian. I don't want it to happen to any other girl. Vivian, can't you stop him? Can't you do something?" Monica pleaded.

Vivian was quiet for a few moments. Monica waited. She didn't know why, but she trusted Vivian.

"I'll see what I can do, Monica." Vivian's face looked hard and angry. "Yeh, Monica, I'm gonna stop fat Maynard."

Vivian sounded more like usual when she stood up and said, "Just leave it to me, Monica. I'm gonna stop that creep."

The next morning Dusty wandered over to Monica's bed. "LP, LP." But as soon as the taunts started, Vivian walked over and looked Dusty in the eye. Vivian was older than

Dusty by about two years, and she stood more than a head taller.

"That's it, Dusty. No more of that LP stuff."

That was all Vivian had to say.

Monica was amazed, but she had seen Vivian in action before. She could be as mean as a cornered wild mother cat, but if she decided something wasn't fair she made sure she straightened the thing out.

And people listened.

4

VIVIAN HAD BEEN AT KUPER LONGER THAN ANYONE HAD. She said she was fifteen and that was probably true, but no one knew for sure. Sister Mary Louise said even the government didn't know exactly how old Vivian was—her mom had forgotten to register her birth, then she had disappeared.

If anyone asked Vivian where she was from, she answered, "I can go home anytime I want. I got people. If you look hard enough, you can see my place over there in Chemainus. But I know what's good for me. This is close enough."

Monica didn't know what she meant. But Vivian never went home. She never got any letters from home and no one ever sent her anything, not even twenty-five cents on her birthday. Vivian didn't go home for Christmas or summer holidays.

Nellie said Vivian's mom and dad had died in a car crash and that she'd seen it all. And that was how she got that big scar on her cheek.

· But Vivian told a different story.

"If you think my cheek looks bad, you should see old nun Nancy's face," Monica had heard Vivian brag in the dining hall. "She caught my cheek with a ruler but I picked up the vase on her desk and hit her right on the forehead. They needed twenty stitches to put her back together.

"That was before any of you guys got here," Vivian continued. "I was only eight or nine years old."

But Monica believed Nellie's story about the car accident because she never heard Vivian say a word about her mom and dad.

It was Vivian who put a stop to everyone teasing Monica. She told Nellie, "From now on no one is going to call Monica LP. And I am going to make sure even fat Maynard shuts his mouth up."

Vivian turned around and announced to the girls as they dressed that morning, "Anyone not hear? Then let me say it again. No one in this dorm is named LP. Got it?"

When Sister Mary Louise came into the room she didn't know what had happened. She looked over at Monica.

"So, LP, you feel better dis morning?" The sister laughed, expecting the others to join in.

The room was silent. Girls shuffled quietly, buttoning their shirts and putting on their socks, heads turned.

"Looks like you feeling better, LP," Sister Mary Louise repeated.

Vivian moved across the room until she was looking Sister Mary Louise right in the eye. "There is no one here by that name. If you are talking to her," Vivian said, nodding her head at Monica, "I suggest you call her Monica." Vivian's back stiffened. "That's her name."

Sister Mary Louise hesitated, a confused look spreading over her face.

"And tell fat Maynard the same thing."

Sister Mary Louise lifted her arms and flapped her hands against her chest. Her eyes darted around the room as she realized all the girls were watching. Vivian moved closer, not taking her eyes off the nun.

"You ... you. ..." The sister struggled to gain control. "His name is Father Maynard, and you go straight to his office for calling him names."

"Glad to, Sister," Vivian answered insolently. "I gotta few things to say to him about names myself."

Vivian slowly finished getting dressed while Sister Mary Louise stood by helplessly.

When Vivian was finished, she turned and said to Sister Mary Louise, "Are you ready? I'm going to see fat Maynard now."

In a fluster, Sister Mary Louise followed Vivian out of the dorm.

Monica, Agnes, Dusty and Nellie lingered outside Father Maynard's office on the way to breakfast and listened for the sound of Vivian's voice. The room was silent.

No one saw Vivian the whole day.

Early that evening, Monica retreated to the dorm to read.

"Have you seen Vivian?" Dusty asked as she charged into the quiet room.

"No, she hasn't been here. I haven't seen her all day," Monica replied.

"Neither has anyone else." Dusty stepped close to Monica's bed. The girls looked at each other.

"Sorry, Monica. Still friends?" Dusty asked.

Monica was quiet for a moment. Then she nodded. "Yeh, still friends. Always."

"Well, friend, I gotta find out what's happened to Vivian."

Dusty headed out as fast as she came in.

Monica smiled.

When the girls started filing into the dorm later, everyone was talking about Vivian. They sat on their beds, discussing what they had heard.

"Not a sound came from Maynard's office this morning."

"Yeh, it didn't even sound like she went there."

"Then where did she go?"

Nellie stood in the centre of the circle. "Well, girls, we gotta do something for her." Now that she had stood up for Monica and told Sister Mary Louise where to go, Vivian was a hero.

Just as Nellie spoke, Sister Mary Louise walked into the room.

Nellie turned to her and shouted, "Where is Vivian? Where did you take her? What have you done with her?"

"Her father came from Victoria, pick her up dis afternoon. She tell Father Maynard she want to leave school." Sister Mary Louise shifted from one foot to the other uncomfortably.

"We know she doesn't have no dad, and if she does, he doesn't live in Victoria," Nellie said hotly. "You've done something to her. We know you have."

"What did Vivian do? What did she say about fat man Maynard?" Dusty demanded. "We know she was planning something, and now you've all gotten rid of her."

Sister Mary Louise looked nervous. Her face was burning red and her hands shook.

"You girls tink you know everyting." Her voice was thin and shaky. "You all so smart. What about you, LP? How smart are you, now dat Vivian, she is gone? Did she make enough trouble for you? She fix it up for you, did she?"

Sister Mary Louise moved away from Nellie and Dusty

and glared at Monica. "Dis is your fault, little troublemaker. If Vivian gone, dis is your fault."

For the first time since Monica arrived at the school, she felt strength creep up her spine. She stood up and, instead of backing away, she stepped toward the sister. At first Monica had no words. She stood silently. Then, to everyone's surprise, she spoke.

"I'm not the trouble, sister. You are. And Father Maynard is. I didn't do anything wrong. Vivian told me that. And Vivian didn't do anything wrong either. Father Maynard is not going to hurt me again, and you aren't going to help him out. Vivian told me Father Maynard will stop hurting me. And if he doesn't, I'm going to tell my dad."

Monica didn't know what had got into her. But she didn't care.

"My dad will cause you a lot of trouble if you hurt me. Or if you hurt Vivian."

She trembled as she sat down.

No one heard anything about Vivian for three days. On the third day, Father Maynard called a special assembly in the chapel. All the students filed in and sat down. After a prolonged silence, he stood up.

His body was heaving up and down with each breath he took. His face was red and swollen, and huge drops of perspiration stained his black gown.

"Children." Father Maynard's knuckles were white as he steadied himself against the pulpit. He cleared a thick clog out of his throat and spat it into his handkerchief. "Children, I have a wonderful announcement. It may seem sad at this moment, but the Lord knows what is best for us all. I have been called away. The Lord has called me to work far away from our school."

He paused, expecting a response. The room remained silent except for his laboured breathing and a slight gasp from Sister Mary Louise. Then he continued.

"It is a wonderful thing that the Lord has called me once again to work in His field. I will be going to another school on the other side of the country. But only for a short time, and then I will return."

Once again he waited. The kids had no reaction.

"I am sad that I must say goodbye for now to all you children and to our great school here on Kuper Island. I will return as soon as my work is complete.

"One final thing," Father Maynard continued. "The Lord has called each and every one of you to work for Him. Let me be an example to you. Listen to His call and follow the Lord."

Everyone remained silent as Father Maynard finished. Then cheers erupted from the back of the boys' side of the chapel. Monica turned around.

Nelson was jumping up on the seat, waving his arms hysterically. "Yippee! The fat man is gone. The fat man is gone. The fat man is gone." Nelson started singing, and then he began to lead the rest of the boys as if he were a choirmaster.

Brother Jerry and Brother Henry Philipe rushed over and pulled Nelson down off his seat. They dragged him out the back door, but he continued to sing at the top of his lungs. You could hear him all the way down the hall.

"Goodbye, fat man! Good riddance, fat man. Glad the Lord called you away."

Father Maynard ignored the ruckus and continued speaking. "I know you all will feel sad today. Goodbyes are always sad. I am already looking forward to my return." Then he sat down.

The girls congregated outside when the assembly was over. Nellie and Dusty stood in the middle of the group.

"I bet this has something to do with Vivian," Nellie said.

"Yeh," Dusty agreed. "It's just too much of a coincidence that the fat man takes a holiday right after Vivian disappears."

"But where is she?"

"How did they get rid of her?"

"And what happened to make Father Maynard leave?"

Everyone had a question, but no one could figure it out.

Then, two weeks after Vivian disappeared, Nellie's Auntie Nora came to visit from Nanaimo.

Sister Mary Louise met Nellie at breakfast.

"I meant to tell you yesterday," she said. "Your Auntie Nora will be here after class today. To visit."

Nellie was excited. Auntie Nora took care of Nellie and her brothers and sisters. And whenever Auntie Nora came to the school, she was like an auntie to all the girls. Monica had never been part of the group before, but this time Nellie wanted her to join in.

"Want to come and meet my auntie?" Nellie asked Monica during lunch break. "You'll really like her."

"Sure," Monica said. She had seen Auntie Nora before and always wished she could talk to her.

Monica waited excitedly during class. When the bell rang, she followed Nellie, Dusty and all the other girls outside and along the wharf. Jim was just pulling in as the girls ran down the steep ramp.

"Auntie! Auntie!" Nellie shrieked as Jim helped the woman out of the boat.

Auntie Nora was a tall woman with long, shiny black hair pulled back in a ponytail and wrapped in a gold scarf. Monica admired her even, white teeth and gracious smile.

The girls danced around Auntie Nora. Everyone wanted to touch her and talk at once.

"Girls, girls, girls! Slow down. I'm gonna stay awhile." Auntie Nora opened her arms and hugged the girls. Monica stepped back from the excited group. She looked up to the sky over the wharf. First she heard and then she saw a huge eagle soaring over the bay where they stood.

"Come here, young lady," Auntie Nora called to Monica. "I haven't met you before. Don't be shy." She beckoned for Monica to move closer. Monica smiled and stepped into the woman's arms.

"You look like you need a hug," she said as she pulled Monica close. "Auntie Nora is here for everyone, you know. I've come over to make sure you are all right."

The group slowly moved up the wharf.

"Nellie." Auntie Nora's face became serious. "I heard there have been some problems over here."

"What have you heard, Auntie?" Nellie said. "We don't even know what is going on, and we live here."

The woman sat down on the cement stairs leading up to the school. The girls encircled her.

"You know, girls, there isn't much I don't hear about. Most people don't believe their ears when they hear the stories from this place. But I went here too. Years ago now. And I remember what it was like.

She looked around furtively to make sure no one was listening. Then she puckered her lips and shook her head.

"I promised Nellie's mom, before she got sick, that I would send Nellie to school. Nellie was just a little girl back then. But I did what I promised. I thought the school had changed. I sent her here because I thought it would be best for her. But I have never trusted this school. I keep my eyes open and my ear to the ground."

"Tell us, Auntie. Tell us what went on. One of our friends is missing, and Father Maynard just up and left for a while. And that's all we know."

"That confirms what I know." The woman nodded and continued. "The girl that's missing is Vivian Rodgers from the Chilliwack area. She was sent to this school when she was five years old. She's been here for more than ten years. She's an orphan."

"Where's Chilliwack? Why is she an orphan?" someone asked.

"Chilliwack's not far from Vancouver. She's an orphan because both her parents died in a car accident. There was no family member to take her in. So the Indian agent brought her over here. This is the only family she has known for all this time."

"We didn't think her story about living in Chemainus was true. No one ever visited her. She never went home for holidays—not even in the summer," Dusty said.

"Well, she's been sent back to her village now, but I doubt she knows anyone there anymore. I heard they just put her on the boat to Vancouver with a bus ticket home. They didn't care if anyone was there to take her into their home."

"Why?" Dusty asked.

"You won't believe what she did." Auntie Nora sounded like one of the girls. "I heard Vivian went right into Father Maynard's room and told him she knew he was abusing one of the girls. She said he had abused her too and that she was going to tell the police. She said she was going to tell everyone who came over to the island.

"Father Maynard got mad and started slapping her around. Vivian must be one strong girl. I heard she wound up and punched him until he was flat on his back on the floor. Then she held a chair up against his throat and told him he better get out or she would kill him."

"How did you find all this out?" Nellie asked.

"Well, a couple of nuns escorted Vivian across to Chemainus to meet the Indian agent. When they got to the dock on the other side, Vivian broke loose from the nuns. My friend Eva Lucille was waiting at the dock and Vivian ran over to her and told her the whole story. Then Vivian ran over to old lady Esther, from the point over in Chemainus, and said the same thing. She asked them both to tell someone and help the girls on Kuper.

"Esther was going to ignore the whole thing, but Eva talked her into going with her to the police station in Chemainus. They told Vivian's story to that police chief. They told him that Father Maynard had abused one too many girls and that they would stop at nothing till the police investigated."

"Wow!" Dusty exclaimed. "What did the police do?"

"They must have come over here and checked it out. I heard they called Eva in to talk on the record. You girls are safe for a while. Thanks to Vivian. But I think I'd better take Nellie home."

"I get to go home!" Nellie looked excited. Then she stood still, confused. "But what about my friends? Do they have to stay?"

"I can't bring you all home. But I think you are safe now. I will stay on the lookout. Don't you girls worry."

Monica wondered if Dad had heard any of the story down in Tsartlip. She decided Dad knew only what she wrote in her letters. Monica quietly left the girls and Auntie Nora. She wandered up the stairs and into the dorm.

She opened her writing pad and found her pen.

Dear Dad,
    I miss you so much today. Things are okay now. I am

feeling better than I was.

I am missing a good friend. She left the school and moved back to Chilliwack. Her name is Vivian. She was an especially good friend to me. I hope I see her sometime. Another friend is leaving today to go home to Nanaimo. Her auntie says she can go to regular high school. Her name is Nellie and I am going to miss her too.

I am working hard at my studies. I am still getting As on everything.

Tell Amelia I miss her too much. And Donnie and Ronnie and Reggie.

Oh, I forgot to tell you. Father Maynard was sent away for a while. I don't know for how long. I can't say that I will miss him.

I sure miss you all.

I am fine now.

Your daughter forever,

> *Monica*

Nelson

1

THE SUN HAD BURNED OFF THE RAIN CLOUDS, AND IT
HAD turned into one of those so-bright-you-need-to-squint
September days, when Agent Macdonald came to the Day
School and dragged the kids off to Kuper Island. Nelson was
confused. The whole thing had caught him off guard. He
would rather have gone duck hunting.

He could have got out of bed that morning, grabbed his
shotgun, thrown on his cap and boots and headed down
to the spit with Dad and Rusty, his German shepherd. He
could have shot a couple of mallards, strung them on a line
and dragged them back to Mom. Then he could have hung
around the kitchen while she plucked off the feathers and

tossed the ducks into a pot with carrots and onions. If he had waited long enough, he could have had a bowl of duck soup and scough bread.

Nelson hated Brother Jerry. He knew it right away, the minute he looked into the brother's face. As thin as Father Maynard was fat, Brother Jerry had eyes that were half closed and guard-dog mean, sitting tightly together on either side of his bony nose. You couldn't trust a face like that.

Howard caught up to Nelson as he followed the brother up the steps to the building.

Nelson turned to him. "Brother Jerry is a creep," he muttered in a low voice. "I can tell just from looking at him."

"Come on, Nelson. Don't start. Try to stay out of trouble for a least a day or two." Howard knew once Nelson got started, no one would be able to get him to quit.

"Do you boys have something you want to say?" Brother Jerry swung around at the top of the stairs to face them. His voice was penetrating and high-pitched and sounded more like a woman's than a man's.

"No, we don't have nothing to say with ya," Nelson blurted out.

"No, we don't have *anything* to say to *you*," Brother Jerry corrected him, emphasizing the words and speaking loudly as if Nelson couldn't hear.

"Oh, you don't have nothing to say with us neither, huh," Nelson lipped back. The brother's pink face darkened to bright red.

"Has no one taught you how to speak English, Nelson?" he sputtered in contempt. "Is that your name? Nelson?"

"Yeh, my name's Nelson. You asked me that already. And my English don't need no correcting."

"Lay off, Nelson," Howard whispered. "At least wait until we find our way around. We don't need this kind of trouble."

"You've got a lot more to correct than just your English, mister smart mouth." The brother's thin white lips were drawn like barricades as he fired words out between his teeth.

When they reached the dorm, Brother Jerry lined the two boys up against the wall. The brother didn't stand much bigger than Howard, Nelson realized, except that he was stooped a little. His shoulders slumped forward, forming a cavity in his chest and sending his neck out in front like a vulture.

"From now on, you will speak when you are spoken to, you will use correct English and you will not talk under your breath. Do you have that perfectly clear?" He repeated himself slowly as his eyes bounced from Howard to Nelson and back again.

Howard nodded his head.

"And what about you?" Brother Jerry's eyes were narrow, only open a slit, and seemed to pierce right into Nelson. "Do you understand my rules?"

He was asking the wrong Indian to understand his rules. Nelson knew about white men's rules. He had heard his dad and Uncle Frankie talking about that very thing just a few days before. They were leaning on the kitchen table after dinner complaining about an argument Uncle Frankie had had in town.

"Those damn white men won't be happy until they have the last Indian dead or doing exactly what they say," Uncle Frankie had said. "What's with white men, anyway? They have rules for everything. They probably can't even take a crap without having some rule for it."

Dad had turned to Nelson once Uncle Frankie finished and said, "Don't let them control you, son. Don't ever let no white man tell you the rules. They make a damn mess of everything they touch."

Nelson stared Brother Jerry right in his eye as Dad and Uncle Frankie's words ran through his mind.

"You are talking to the wrong Indian if you are talking about rules," Nelson said defiantly.

Brother Jerry squinted even more and took a step toward Nelson. He reached out and, with one hand, cuffed Nelson hard up the side of his head, knocking him flying back onto a bed.

One second after he hit the bed, he sprang back up, jumped right on top of Brother Jerry and threw him down onto his back. Then Nelson hit him hard with a right punch, and another with the left. Just as he got the brother pinned, Howard grabbed Nelson's shirt and yanked. He pulled Nelson off Brother Jerry then sat on Nelson's legs and tried to hold on to his arms until he calmed down.

"Quit now, Nelson. Just quit now," Howard said, trying to catch his breath. "Why don't you just leave it alone?"

Brother Jerry slowly rolled over till his feet touched the floor, then he stood up. He held his jaw with one hand as he opened his mouth wide. Then he combed his fingers through his hair and readjusted his black gown. He took a deep breath followed by another, stood still for a moment or two and then turned to Nelson.

"Nelson," he said in a quavering voice. He shook his arms and legs out, like Mom did when she hung the clothes on the line. "That will be the last time you ever try that on me. You better be thankful that I am going to keep this altercation to myself. But you won't get a second chance. I won't forget. I will make your life miserable."

With that Brother Jerry turned around and walked out of the room. Howard released Nelson's arms and slipped off his lap. The boys sat together for a few moments.

"You won't get another chance either, you creep," Nelson mumbled under his breath. "And I won't forget."

"That guy's mean, Nelson. Really mean." Howard shook his head. "And now look what you've done. We were supposed to get our beds and our clothes." He stood up and peered out the door and down the hall.

Nelson lay back on the bed and stared at the ceiling.

"Ya wanna know something, Howard? Do ya wanna know what I think about this place?" Nelson stalled for a minute while he tried to put his thoughts and feelings into words. He started thinking of Dad and Uncle Frankie again.

"Yeh, I do, Nelson. I wanna know what you think of this place." Howard sat down and waited for him to answer.

"First, I gotta say that this whole thing's caught me by surprise." Nelson tried again to put his thoughts together. "It's getting clear now, though. I figure they got us in this place to hold us down and squeeze every bit of Indian out of us."

At first it didn't make much sense, even to Nelson, once he said the words.

"Really, Nelson? Why do you think that?"

"It's not about why I think it. It's about what we are going to be like if they do it. What if they squeeze all the Indian out of us? What'll be left? What do they want, Howard? We're Indians. That's it. That's what we are." Nelson didn't know where the words came from, but in a way, he knew he had it right.

He stared at the ceiling. The traces of a thin paintbrush created pale green criss-cross patterns on the wooden slats. Nelson's mind wandered. Maybe the painter hadn't had quite enough paint. He imagined a man stretching up from a not-quite-high-enough scaffold and swishing the ceiling with the tip of his brush.

2

As Nelson changed for bed the first night, one boy came up to him in the dorm and then another.

"Hey. You the guy that pinned Brother Jerry on the bed and scared the heck out of him?"

"I hear you beat up Brother Jerry."

The word had got around quickly.

Once the lights were out, moonlight allowed Nelson to focus his eyes again on the paint patterns on the ceiling. They looked like fish netting behind the eerie shadows cast by the autumn moon. Except for a few whispers and snorts as one boy after the other fell off to sleep, the room was quiet.

But soon Nelson was aware of a conversation coming from the corner.

"Marty. Did ya hear about the tough guy from Tsartlip? Thinks he can take on Brother Jerry the first day."

"Yeh, man, I heard."

"What are you going to do about it?" Someone else piped in.

"I guess I'll find out how tough he is." Nelson began to distinguish which voice was Marty's. Marty was obviously the tough guy.

"I'll see what he's made of." Marty snorted a contemptuous laugh and the other guys snickered.

Nelson breathed in deeply and held on to the sides of his mattress. He wanted to jump up and grab Marty whoever-he-thought-he-was by his sissy pajamas. Nelson was ready to fight. But instead he lay perfectly still. Not yet, he thought. Wait until you can see what you're fighting.

Nelson thought of fights he had seen—mostly with Dad and Uncle Frankie downtown. He drifted into a half-sleep as his mind wandered back home. He was sitting in the worn red leather back seat of Uncle Frankie's '42 Plymouth on the way home from the Drake Hotel. Dad and Uncle Frankie were brave from whiskey and mad from insults. Both were beat up black and blue.

"Sometimes a man's just gotta stick up for himself," Dad had said.

"Did ya hear that, nephew?" Uncle Frankie had twisted around—one hand on the steering wheel, the other pointing at Nelson. "Did ya hear what your Dad's telling ya?"

"You listen up, boy. Listen up to your old man. You don't let no one push you around. Not no white man. Not no Indian. You watch your old man and your Uncle Frankie, they know how to stick up for themselves."

Nelson slipped into a dream. The sun etched orange, red and yellow streaks across the sky above James Island. The spit was still grey and misty from the cool night. Dad and Nelson sat crouched in the long grass and waited for the ducks. . . .

The next morning Nelson woke early. The sun was already bright and the room was warm. The room also seemed quiet. Boys spoke in a hush and he could feel that something was going on. He watched the boys look him up and down as he walked toward the washroom to wash up.

As Nelson turned to leave the washroom, a boy leaned against the door and blocked his way. He dipped his finger into the basin and flicked water into Nelson's face.

Nelson slowly wiped himself with his towel. The boy moved a little closer, until his elbow poked into Nelson's side.

"So ya took on Brother Jerry, huh," the boy mumbled under his breath.

Nelson kept drying the same spot. "Yeh. What about it?"

He pushed hard into Nelson's ribs. Nelson pulled away

and studied the boy. They were both about the same size, but the other boy looked a little older than Nelson's 14 years. He was lean with wide shoulders and muscled, bowed legs. He stood confidently with his jaw extended sharply, accentuating his piercing eyes. A thick, red scar started at his left ear and cut deeply into his cheek almost to his nose.

Nelson dropped his towel in the basin and turned. He pressed his shoulder into the boy, shoved him aside and walked down the corridor to the dorm.

The boy followed close behind. "Tough guy, eh. Think you can take me on, do you?" he called out.

Nelson turned and said, "I'll take on whoever gets in my way."

"After class. Behind the gym. And I'm Marty, by the way."

"I'll be there."

Howard heard them as they entered the dorm. "Gawd, Nelson. Do you have to?"

"Yeh, Howard, I have to."

After class Howard and Nelson met in the corridor.

Howard was agitated. "Nelson, maybe you could talk to him. Tell him you don't want to fight him. Did ya see how tough he looks?"

"Yeh, I saw, you numbskull. Do ya think I'm blind? He was shoving me around in the washroom. I didn't make no mistake. Brother Jerry ain't pushing me around and Marty ain't gonna neither. Are you coming with me or am I going on my own?"

Nelson headed toward the back door. Howard reluctantly followed him a few paces behind.

The gym, a large red wood building surrounded by mature maples and oaks, stood high on a rock outcropping behind the school.

The boys followed the worn dirt path encircling the

building until they heard laughter. They slowed down, then stopped for a few seconds, before Nelson continued. Howard stayed safely back.

A group of least ten boys stood in a huddle. They all turned at once and looked at Nelson as he rounded the corner. The laughter subsided until there wasn't a sound.

Nelson took a deep breath. His eyes darted from one boy to the other, assessing the situation, and then he stepped forward and said, "Takes ten guys, hey, Marty?"

Marty swaggered out from the centre of the group, took a long drag from his cigarette and flicked it on the ground. He lifted the toe of his boot and slowly, deliberately, ground the sizzling ash into the mud.

"It takes one. Punk. These guys are here to watch you get beat."

Marty stepped closer and then stood, legs apart, shifting from one foot to the other. Each thumb was hooked into a back pocket of his pants. Nelson looked closely at his face. Marty had been in fights before. His nose was bent in the centre and then flattened, spreading his nostrils unnaturally wide. The scar now looked blue, almost black, and foreboding. One eyebrow was slightly swollen, giving the impression of a permanent scowl.

"Pssst. Let's get out of here." Howard poked his head around the corner and tried to get Nelson's attention.

"Just tell me when you're ready, boy scout," Marty sneered.

Nelson looked past him to the crowd standing behind.

"He's all yours, Marty."

"Go get him, Marty."

Their voices became vague and drawn, stretched like elastic reaching Nelson from a distant horizon.

Then Nelson caught a glimpse of Brother Jerry off to the

side of the group, leaning against a giant oak. He felt a surge of energy. For a split second his mind cleared.

He took a step closer to Marty until he saw beads of sweat forming on the hairs on the other boy's tight upper lip. Nelson inhaled. Marty reeked of musty sweat and smoke.

The next thing Nelson knew he was face down in the mud. Marty stabbed his knee into Nelson's back and squeezed his hand over the back of his head, slowly twisting his face into the ground.

Razor-sharp pains shot up through his nose and into his brain. He gasped for breath, but instead his mouth filled with mud and stones mixed with blood. He kicked his legs and wildly swung his arms around to break free, but Marty had him pinned.

"Eat mud, Tsartlip. Chew it up. That's all you're going to get to eat for a while," Marty shouted as the other guys cheered him on. The more the crowd shouted, the harder Marty pushed Nelson's face into the ground. The whirl of pain and blood and jeers spun around. It seemed like forever. There was nothing he could do.

Then, out of somewhere deep inside, the pain and fear turned to rage. Power surged through Nelson's legs and arms like a wave washing over him. The louder the crowd laughed the stronger he felt. Without any warning, he twisted his body and flung Marty onto the ground.

Nelson scrambled to his feet, wiped the blood off his chin and spat a big wad of mud toward the crowd. Then he turned on Marty. He kicked and punched like a madman. Everyone was quiet as he pinned down Marty's squirming body. Nelson leaned his elbow into the other boy's back and held him for a moment. He felt light as a feather and powerful as a giant.

For a second, he didn't know what to do next. The crowd

was stunned. They stood silent and stared down at Marty sprawled out in the mud.

Without another thought, Nelson stood up and took off back down the path and into the school. Howard ran behind him. He checked over his shoulder to see if anyone else followed. No one.

When they reached the dorm, panting and out of breath, the two boys collapsed on the bed.

"Geez, Nelson, you really got that guy!" Howard exclaimed and then paused. "But now what's gonna happen?"

Nelson fell back onto the bed and punched into the air. He was proud and scared at the same time. Half of him expected ten guys to blast into the room at any minute and plaster his body against the wall. The other half was high on elation from the victory. Flying.

"What'll happen now, Howard? No one in this school will be dumb enough to fight with me again."

Something had changed inside Nelson while his face was smashed in the mud. He had watched himself turn his rage and humiliation into power. He was a fighter. He knew it now.

Marty knew it too. Along with the rest of the guys.

Then Nelson remembered Brother Jerry, leaning against the tree.

Watching.

3

NELSON DIDN'T HAVE MUCH TO DO WITH HOWARD AFTER that. Everything changed. He became one of the crowd.

Marty was sent home a few weeks after the fight. Graduated. That's what they said. Nelson found out later that graduation meant you were too old or too tough to stay at the school. A guy could graduate from Kuper after ten years, even if he had only a grade three education.

The day Marty caught the boat, all the guys headed down the wharf with him. They crowded around the *Monfort*, cuffing Marty and slapping him on the back.

"Good luck, tough guy. Give it to them."

"Hey, man," Marty said as he stepped into the boat. He offered his hand to Nelson. "Take over, man. It's all yours. Don't let anyone push you around."

The two boys shook hands while the crowd watched. Soon the boat took off with Marty, and the boys walked quietly back up to the school.

From that day on Nelson took his rightful place as the leader of the crowd. Nelson made sure any new students and younger boys knew who was boss. He started smoking, although at first it hurt his throat. Inhaling the smoke often made him choke, but he learned to cough discreetly so the other boys didn't catch on.

Being the tough guy at Kuper had its advantages. No one challenged Nelson much as he swaggered down the corridors with his collar turned up and his thumbs placed deliberately in his pants pockets.

Rosy and the other senior girls met the crowd in the schoolyard and exchanged glances and smiles—sometimes more, if Brother Jerry wasn't patrolling. The guys said Rosy had been Marty's girl, but it looked to Nelson that she was over him. She winked and blew Nelson a kiss. Nice payoff, he thought as he eyed Rosy's chocolate-coloured curls bouncing softly in the sunlight. She hiked her skirt up a bit shorter than the other girls and rolled her socks down over her shoes, exposing her thin, shapely legs.

"Get out of here, you animals. You aren't allowed to talk to the girls during recess." Brother Jerry shoved the boys away from the girls. "Let's go, girls. You don't want to talk to these beasts.

"You touch one of them and I'll have your butt, mister smart mouth." Brother Jerry spit the words out under his breath as he passed Nelson.

Brother Jerry watched every move Nelson made.

One morning before Thanksgiving, Nelson and the crowd were heading to class after having a smoke. As usual, Brother Jerry was waiting in the hall. Most of the students were already sitting in their desks when the boys filed, one by one, past the door and sat down in their desks.

Nelson was the last one in. As he passed Brother Jerry, the brother eyed him up and down. Just as he was about to sit down in his desk, Brother Jerry strode across the room and blocked the seat.

"You're late," the brother shouted at the top of his lungs. "It is 9:05. Class starts at 9:00 sharp."

"Hey, man," Nelson snickered. "What's with the bad mood? What's five minutes? Look here, Rosy isn't even sitting down yet."

Rosy came in the door after Nelson and snuck behind Brother Jerry and sat at her desk. She never got in trouble for anything.

"Shut up, boy!" Brother Jerry barked. "You think you can get away with anything here. You think you are such a tough guy. Well, in this class, you are going to learn that I am the boss. I am the tough guy."

"Easy, easy, easy, big guy."

"Easy? You want me to be easy. What are you . . . a baby?" Brother Jerry stepped toward Nelson.

Instinctively, Nelson held up his arm just as the brother swung a yardstick right at his face. The stick hit his forearm and shattered, sending one piece across the room and right out the window.

"Get out of here!" Brother Jerry shrieked. "You get out of here! Father Maynard is going to deal with you. I have had it!"

He grabbed Nelson's shirt and pulled him into the corridor.

"Lay off, you creep." Nelson struggled to stay on his feet as the brother yanked and shoved him. "Back off already. I'm coming."

When Nelson swung around to break free from his grip, the brother let go, tripped, then fell hard against the wall.

Everything went from bad to worse. Brother Jerry was ready to explode by the time the two reached Father Maynard's office. His face was red and sweating, and tears welled up in his eyes.

"Nelson hit me in front of the class and then knocked me down in the hall," he stammered to Father Maynard. "I have had all I can take of him."

"Son." Father Maynard glared at Nelson as he slowly opened the top drawer of his desk. He carefully removed a long, thick, wide leather strap. "We have had nothing but trouble with you since you stepped off that boat."

Father Maynard caressed the strap back and forth in his hands.

"Nelson," he said sternly, "we don't put up with your attitude around here. You are going to get this strap until you learn your lesson. Do you understand?"

"Yes, sir." Just agree, Nelson thought. It'll get it over with.

"I want you to apologize to Brother Jerry for your violent behaviour."

Nelson held his breath and bit his lip. "Yes, sir. I apologize."

He could hardly spit the words out.

"Is that all you have to say?" Father Maynard wasn't satisfied.

"I got nothing else to say," Nelson mumbled sullenly. "I said I was sorry."

"Well, if that's all you have to say, then you really will be sorry." Father Maynard waved the strap back and forth in front of his face. "Lay your arms across the desk."

He had no choice. He stepped forward and plopped his hands down. Father Maynard yanked his fingers until his whole arms were lying flat across the desk. The father wound up and slapped the strap across the boy's hands. Then again. And again. Soon Father Maynard was strapping Nelson's forearm. Then he was hitting the boy all the way up to his short shirt sleeves.

"Make him cry, Father," Brother Jerry yelled.

Nelson clenched his teeth and closed his eyes. He promised himself he would not cry.

Smack. Smack. Smack. Nelson didn't flinch. Finally Father Maynard pulled the strap back and hesitated. Nelson opened his eyes and looked down at his arms. Red and blue welts wound their way around his arms like a barber pole. A thin trickle of blood dribbled down onto the desk.

"That's enough. Now you get out of here. And I don't want to hear from you again. You understand?" Father Maynard's face was red. Beads of sweat stood out on his forehead and upper lip.

Nelson didn't say a word. He raised his head, straightened his back and looked Brother Jerry in the eye as he left the office. He walked down the hall with his arms hanging limply at his sides—burning like they were on fire. His fingers swelled up like wieners.

No one said a word when Nelson entered the classroom.

They stared at his arms as he carefully laid them down on the desk. But he didn't see the others stare. His whole being was alive with rage and at the heart of that anger was the smirking face of Brother Jerry.

Nelson couldn't write for a week. He couldn't pick up a fork or spoon to feed himself. Brother Jerry let Howard help him with his school work.

When Nelson's arms and hands healed over, a wide stripe of rippled blue scar ran down his forearms. He decided to keep his distance from Brother Jerry for a while. He knew they weren't through with each other, but he wasn't in the mood to pick a fight.

Once again school developed a routine. Smokes, class, eat, fight, eat, smokes . . . one day blended into another. Slowly, home came to seem a faraway place. Nelson no longer thought about going home. He received no word from his parents. He didn't know whether they were alive or dead. Sometimes he didn't know if he cared.

It wasn't until after Christmas holidays, the year Nelson was fifteen, that something really different happened. Nelson stayed at the school through the holidays. No one sent for him. Father Maynard said they couldn't get hold of his parents. The holidays were boring and Nelson waited for the other boys to return to the school.

The first morning after the holiday the students filed into the classroom as usual. A young man, dressed like the other brothers, stood outside the door. He was big—at least a head taller than anyone. He had broad shoulders, thick arms and the biggest hands Nelson had ever seen.

The man nodded and smiled at each student as they passed him. "Morning. Morning. Morning."

Everyone settled in their seats, and Brother Jerry and the young man stood in front of the class.

"Good morning," Brother Jerry began. "We have a new addition to our teaching staff. Let me introduce you to Brother Feldstar. Brother Feldstar is going to teach you English and PE."

"Thanks." The young man smiled at the students. "Morning. I'm Leyland Feldstar and I come from Saskatchewan. There, they just call me Feldstar, and that's okay with me."

He sat on the desk. "This is my first teaching job. I am pretty happy to be here in this beautiful place on the West Coast."

Nelson watched him closely. He moved with confidence and ease. He looked genuinely excited about teaching.

"There are two things I really enjoy," he continued. "One is reading and the other is playing soccer. The only trouble with living in Saskatchewan is that it's too cold to play soccer for half the year and too hot the other half. So I expect you guys will teach me a few things."

The next day Feldstar took the boys out to the field.

"Okay," he said as he lined them up. "Tell me the most important thing about playing soccer."

"Getting a goal," someone shouted out from the line.

"No," he answered.

"Checking," someone else guessed.

"No." He waited for a while. "Thinking."

Nelson hardly heard anyone talk about thinking—not at Kuper. And he had *never* heard about thinking when it came to soccer.

"That's right," Feldstar said with a smile. "Surprised? The second thing is hard work. Soccer is about thinking and working. I heard that you Kuper Island soccer players are great, but we are going to make you legendary."

Then, all of a sudden, he was off and running. "Let's go!" he shouted. He ran around the field in front of everyone. "Let's go, you grandmas! What's holding you back?"

As Nelson rounded the third lap, his stomach seized up and he thought he was going to puke. His legs began to cramp, and a sharp piercing pain jolted through his chest.

"It's gotta hurt," Feldstar called back to the boys, "or it's not worth it."

Nelson trained his eye on the teacher. Feldstar ran like a deer—graceful in spite of his size.

After five or six laps, Nelson felt the pain begin to disappear. One leg followed the other. His stomach settled down and he began to float freely between his mind and his body. He imagined leaping through the woods—light, wild.

He didn't take his eyes off Feldstar. When the teacher sped up, Nelson sped up. Feldstar ran faster and faster. Nelson kept pace—right behind him.

Nelson looked around to check out the rest of the guys. They had all collapsed on the sidelines and were watching Feldstar and Nelson circling the field.

Finally Feldstar slowed as they neared the students after the tenth lap. He waited for Nelson.

"Nelson? Is that your name, Nelson?" He patted the boy on the back.

"Yeh. That's me," Nelson replied, panting.

"You are some runner, Nelson. You've got good speed and stamina, and you've got great style."

Nelson hung his head and stared at the muddy field.

"No one ever told you that before?"

"No."

"You know what you really got, Nelson?" Feldstar continued.

"No."

"You got guts."

Nelson lifted his head. "Yeh?"

Nelson wasn't used to compliments. They felt uncomfortable, like he was wearing girls' clothes.

"Yeh. I'm looking forward to working with you."

By the end of January, Nelson was running every day after class. Some days, Feldstar ran with him.

"Hurry up, Nelson," he called. "Push yourself."

Sometimes Nelson wanted to get mad. *Shut up and stop telling me what to do,* he wanted to shout back at Feldstar. But something inside told Nelson that Feldstar could be trusted and that he should listen.

One afternoon, when Nelson was jogging around the field, he heard Brother Jerry's familiar laugh. Nelson tried to ignore him.

"Nelson. Think you're going pretty good, eh," he called out. He waited for Nelson to circle the track. "That Brother Feldstar's putting big ideas in your head."

Nelson sped up around the track. When he passed the brother for the third time, Brother Jerry called out, "You're nothing, Nelson. Nothing."

Nelson boiled inside with rage. He kept his eyes on the track.

The next time around the track, Brother Jerry called out again. "Watch out, Nelson. You get out of line once and I'll have you pulled from the track and PE. Just once and I'll get you."

Nelson clenched his teeth. He wanted to pull off the track and take the brother down right there in the mud. I could beat him, Nelson thought. I have to beat him. Nelson felt his control slipping away. I gotta get him. Before he gets me.

By the time Nelson rounded the track again, Brother Jerry was gone and Feldstar waited on the sidelines. Nelson ran up to him, panting heavily.

"I don't think I'm gonna train this afternoon. I'm not into it today." Nelson kicked a clump of mud.

Feldstar put both his hands on Nelson's shoulders.

"Look at me, Nelson," he said.

Slowly, Nelson lifted his head.

"Don't let him get to you. He wants you to start a fight so he can pull you from training. Remember that being an athlete is all in your mind. Don't let him get to your head. Don't let him win." He patted Nelson on the back and walked away. "Go take a shower," he called behind him.

When Nelson got back to the dorm he flopped on his bed and stared at the patterns on the ceiling. It had been a long time since he thought about Dad and Uncle Frankie, but something brought their words to his mind. "Did you hear that, son? You listen to your dad. Don't you let nobody push you around. You fight, son. You fight."

Then he remembered something Feldstar had told him. "Don't fight him, Nelson. He'll win. He can take away what you want most."

Nelson wanted more than anything to continue training, but he didn't know how long he would be able to control his rage against Brother Jerry.

4

By March, Feldstar had the whole class practising for soccer and track and field. The senior boys and girls were preparing for the upcoming sports days in the villages.

"We will be travelling to three sports days this year," Feldstar announced at the end of March. "Chemainus, Nanaimo and Tsartlip have invited us to compete with them."

Nelson doubled his training time. When the spring days

got longer, he ran after supper while it was still light. He
stopped smoking. First thing every morning, he did one hundred sit-ups. At night, he did as many push-ups as his body
would take. Gradually his body got stronger, more taut. The
other boys prepared by playing soccer, but Nelson spent most
of his time running.

One day, Feldstar took Nelson aside. "We have exactly two
weeks to train before the track meet in Tsartlip. Nelson, you
are the best runner this school has ever seen. And you may
be the best runner for your age in the province. We are going
to go to the top."

Nelson had trouble believing Feldstar. But deep down
inside, Nelson hoped he was right.

On May 17th at 7:00 a.m., Brother Jerry and Feldstar, along
with twenty-three students, filed onto boats and headed to
Chemainus. A long yellow school bus was waiting for them
there.

Brother Jerry stood behind the bus driver as each student
walked past to find a seat.

"Quiet!" he shouted when everyone finally sat down. "I am
going to repeat the arrangements one more time. Listen. We
will arrive at Tsartlip around eleven o'clock. The soccer game
will start after lunch. After the game, all the students from
Tsartlip will be allowed to go home for the night. The rest of
you will go to your billets. Feldstar and I will help you find
your way. Tomorrow morning the track meet starts at 9:00 a.m.
sharp. Make sure you are at the Day School by 8:30."

The soccer game was a wipeout. Before halftime Kuper
Island was ahead six to one. And if Howard hadn't kicked
the ball into the Kuper net, the score would have been six to
zero.

Feldstar huddled the team. "Look, guys. This isn't much of a competition. Back off and let them find their game."

The final score was nine to two.

After the game Sister Theresa brought out large trays of hot dogs and pitchers of orange drink. She set them on a picnic table with mustard, ketchup and relish. After everyone ate, the group dispersed for the night.

Nelson headed home, but he knew no one was going to be there. He hadn't told them he was coming—he hadn't written to or heard from his parents since the summer. Nelson sat for a while at the kitchen table, then sprawled out on the couch, but pretty soon he got bored. He got up and walked around the reserve. Home, he thought to himself. This is home. It didn't feel much like home. But did that mean that Kuper was home? He hoped not.

Nelson kept pretty much to himself. No one seemed to recognize him anyway. It was still light out when he walked back to the house and headed to bed. He fell asleep right away, but he woke up soon after and spent the rest of the night tossing and worrying about the races.

Nelson was the first to arrive at the Day School. The sun was already warm and the sky was clear blue. Not a cloud anywhere—a perfect day for a track meet.

He sat on the fence near the woods and looked across the inlet to the mountains above the Malahat. His eye followed the outline of the mountaintops, tracing the profile of a woman lying on her back—her forehead, nose, chin and neck scooping up over large, round breasts and mounded belly. He wondered why he had never noticed her before.

He looked down at the school building. It seemed small—so different from the building he remembered. White paint peeled off the siding and the once-black windowsills, now flaked and charcoal grey, sank in the corners and separated slightly from the building. Four rooms. No stairs, no dining hall, no chapel. Nelson thought back to the morning he was herded into the black car and taken to Kuper. It was a lifetime ago. Tsartlip was home all right, but he didn't feel like he belonged anymore.

Nelson's cousin Olie walked over, interrupting his thoughts.

"Hey, Nelson. How's it going?"

"Okay. How's it going with you?" Nelson had seen him during the soccer game but avoided talking to him.

"You guys smoked us yesterday, eh?"

"Yeh. You played a good game. But I can't say that for the rest of your team. What's it like back here?"

"Soccer's pretty lame. Especially for us older boys. You oughta see Sister Theresa on the soccer field." Olie laughed. "But wait for today. We got some pretty good runners. Sister Theresa's really into track and field."

Nelson couldn't imagine it, but he smiled back.

"She has me out on the track every day. I hear you are running these days too, eh, cuz?"

"Yeh. I've been running for a few months."

"Sister Theresa says it's gonna be me against you."

"You're kidding. My cuz is going to take me on?" Nelson was surprised. He hadn't thought of who would be his competition. If he had, he never would have guessed his little cousin Olie.

"See you at the races," Olie said. He jumped off the fence and headed in the direction of the school. Nelson followed a few steps behind.

A small crowd had gathered around Sister Theresa and Brother Jerry. She was printing the program on a chalkboard propped up on an old wooden frame at the side of the field.

RACES	JUMPING
100 YARDS	LONG JUMP
220 YARDS	HIGH JUMP
440 YARDS	TRIPLE JUMP
880 YARDS	
CROSS-COUNTRY	

Nelson could see that Brother Jerry and Sister Theresa disagreed about the program.

"I thought that each student could enter only two events," Brother Jerry said, his lips pulled tight.

"No. I don't know where you would get that from," Sister Theresa replied.

"We should be fair to all the students. Everyone deserves a chance to win," he insisted.

"We will be fair, Brother Jerry. But how do you think that would be accomplished by forcing students to sit on the sidelines?"

There's only one guy he wants to sit on the sidelines, and that's me, Nelson thought.

But Sister Theresa wasn't about to let Brother Jerry make the rules. "I don't know what you are worried about, brother." She was oblivious to his ulterior motive. "We will make sure every student gets a fair chance."

Brother Jerry retreated.

Sister Theresa finished printing the program then picked up the orange megaphone.

"Attention, children. Attention, children." She waited a few seconds and then, in her usual way of repeating herself, said it a third time. "Attention, children."

Everyone quieted down.

"The events are posted on the board, and there are sign-up sheets on the table. I want the athletes to sign up for all the events they wish to enter."

The crowd began to shift over to the table, and, one by one, everyone stepped up to the paper. Olie was at the front of the line. Nelson watched him sign his name at least three times. Nelson studied his cousin as he turned from the table. He was short with lean, muscled legs and had the sleek upper body of an athlete. He walked lightly and held his head up, as if his body and mind were a finely tuned instrument.

When Nelson got to the table he quickly scanned the paper for Olie's name. 'Olie' was neatly printed under every senior boys' running event.

Nelson added his own name. Then he sat with the crowd near the far end of the field. Rosy had saved a spot for him.

"You're gonna win, Nelson. We all know it."

Nelson kept his eye on Olie, pacing alone off to the side.

"Senior boys' 100 yard straight race," Sister Theresa announced. Eight boys headed toward the white chalk line: Richmond, Lester and Nelson from Kuper Island, and five boys from Tsartlip, including Olie. Nelson found a spot in the middle of the track. He kicked at a clump of grass to make a clearing for his foot. Olie waited until all the boys had positioned themselves before taking his place next to Nelson on the right.

As the excited spectators headed over to the finish line, Nelson worked on smoothing out the ground for his start. He watched Olie out of the corner of his eye as he slowly stretched his legs and arms and breathed deliberately in and out. Then he turned his attention to the yellow tape at the end of the field and tried to ignore his cousin. Sister Theresa held one end of the tape and Sister Madeleine held the other.

"Olie! Olie! Olie!" The Day School kids and sisters shouted, repeating the chant in sets of three.

Feldstar moved down the sideline toward the runners. He

held the starting gun high above his head.

"Are you ready?" he called. The sound of his voice calmed Nelson's unsettled stomach.

"Get set." Nelson crouched down.

"Go!" The gun blasted.

Nelson took off. The perfect start. Everything mixed into a blur. He stared straight ahead, focused on the finish line. Seconds later he took it. The yellow tape wrapped around his chest as he flew across the line.

"Way to go, Nelson!" Feldstar hurried to him. He patted the boy's back enthusiastically. "It's a blue ribbon."

Rosy had been assigned the job of giving out the first-place ribbons.

"Nelson! You did it. Told you so," she laughed as she pinned the blue ribbon on his shirt.

The crowd gathered around, slapping Nelson's back and cuffing his head.

"You are great. Way to go, man. You did it for us. We're the best!"

It felt good. Nelson figured he could get used to all the attention. He nodded first one way and then the other. Then he gave the crowd the thumbs-up.

Rosy's friend Mabel pinned the second-place red ribbon on Olie's shirt.

"Good race, cuz," Olie said politely as he passed Nelson.

Nelson needed to find a quiet place to calm down. He wasn't sure how close Olie had been. And he didn't want to ask. He didn't like the competition. His lungs tightened and he could hear his heart pounding.

Nelson didn't pay much attention to the little kids' races and the jumping events. Instead he watched his cousin pace, alone, silently, up and down the sidelines. It unnerved Nelson. Olie looked calm and focused.

"Senior boys' 220 yard race," Sister Theresa called.

The 220 yard was almost a repeat of the 100 yard race. Olie waited for all the runners to find their spots then positioned himself once again on Nelson's right. Nelson got off to another good start. After the first 100 yards he glanced over his shoulder. Olie was about ten paces behind. A few yards later he looked again. Olie had narrowed the distance to four or five paces.

When Nelson took the yellow tape, Olie followed close behind.

Nelson could feel his legs stiffening up. He was getting tired. But when the 440 yard race was run he took it again. This time Olie was only a pace or two behind. Nelson could feel him breathing down his neck.

As Rosy pinned another blue ribbon onto his shirt, Nelson glanced over to the maple tree at the end of the track. Brother Jerry was leaning against the tree. He cupped his hands around his mouth and called out, "He's on to you, Nelson. No chance next race."

Nelson became agitated. He could feel his anger growing in spite of all the cheers from the spectators.

"Okay, Nelson." Feldstar put his hands on Nelson's shoulders and pulled him away from the crowd. "You gotta focus. Olie's a great runner—he's your challenge. Competition is a good thing. It's what you need."

"Olie's right on my tail. And he's gaining on me."

"He's a long-distance runner and he is in good condition."

"But I'm a long-distance runner and the next two events are mine. It's what I've trained for."

"You're right. And you'll take them if you focus. Remember it's all in your head. Don't let him get to you. Keep your mind on your race." The coach slapped Nelson on the back and walked away.

Nelson surveyed the scene. The crowd of spectators was growing with each race. Parents arrived with small children. Old people sat on blankets on the grass. The Day School students ran around noisily.

The Kuper Island students cheered for each other. Rosy and a few of the other girls formed a cheerleading group. They stood in a line, clapped their hands and sang at the top of their lungs.

"One, two, three, four. Who are we for. Nelson, Nelson. Rah, rah, rah!"

Nelson wished everyone would just be quiet or go away. He wanted to run. That was all. And he wanted to win. It was him against Olie. He forced himself to avoid looking at the maple and Brother Jerry leaning against it. But the more he thought about it the harder it was.

He looked over at Sister Theresa. She had pulled Olie away from the crowd. Olie was nodding and smiling at the sister.

"So, what do you think, smart mouth?"

Nelson turned. Brother Jerry was standing right behind him.

"You know," he continued, "I always thought it was a waste of time trying to teach you anything. I always said you'd amount to nothing. And, what do you know—it looks like I'm going to be right. I hear your cousin is the strongest in the 880 and the cross-country. And he's already breathing down your neck."

Nelson refused to answer. He felt his hands curl into fists.

"I guess you're not so tough after all, are you, Nelson. He's gonna be all over you. He's got concentration. The guy has style."

And then Feldstar was by Nelson's shoulder. "That's right, Brother Jerry. Olie has style—the same style as Nelson, don't you think? It must run in the family."

Feldstar put a hand on Nelson's back and gently guided him away from Brother Jerry. Nelson was beside himself with rage.

"Settle down, Nelson," Feldstar said quietly, just as Sister Theresa called the senior boys to the starting line for the 880 yard race. "Remember what we've talked about."

Nelson walked to the start line and took his usual spot in the centre. He glanced over at the maple tree. Brother Jerry was once again leaning against the thick trunk, smirking at Nelson.

A knot formed in his gut. He wanted to run across the field, jump on Brother Jerry . . . bring him down.

Stop it, Nelson said to himself. Calm down. Don't let him win. Don't let him win.

Olie was preparing for the race just like he had for the first two races—quietly, calmly.

Feldstar lifted the starting gun. "Attention, boys."

He waited for the runners to settle down.

"880 yards is four laps around the field. Pace yourself."

"Are you ready?" Nelson tensed.

"GO!"

The gun went off before Nelson had time to think. He took off as fast as he could.

Think. He tried to calm himself.

Nelson looked over his shoulder as he completed the first lap. Olie was about five yards behind—running easily.

Feldstar called from the sideline as Nelson passed him. "Pace yourself, Nelson. Concentrate."

His mind settled down as he rounded the second lap. He looked back and saw that most of the runners had fallen way back, but Olie was still running five yards behind. In the third lap there was no change.

"Nelson! Nelson! Nelson! Nelson!" Rosy and the cheerleaders were chanting. Nelson gave them the thumbs-up as he approached the last turn. He felt confident. He smiled at the crowd. When he pulled out of the final turn Nelson saw the yellow tape at the end of the last straight stretch.

Suddenly he could hear Olie's feet pounding on the outside lane.

Shocked, Nelson glanced back. Olie was less than three paces behind him. In four paces Olie was ahead—as if he had turned on an auxiliary motor. Nothing could stop him. He passed Nelson like a shot. Olie pressed his chest out and took the yellow tape five paces ahead of his cousin.

The crowd erupted. Everyone crowded around Olie. Sister Theresa hugged him and even Rosy ran over and congratulated him as she pinned the blue ribbon to his shirt.

Nelson collapsed on the grass. His heart was pounding like a drum as he lay back and closed his eyes. When he opened his eyes, Brother Jerry was looming over him.

"He got you, Nelson. Best run I've seen all day. That boy is amazing."

Seething, Nelson jumped up. He grabbed Brother Jerry just as Feldstar arrived.

"Good race." Quickly he pulled Nelson back. "Pacing and concentration. You just lost your pacing and your concentration on the last lap. Olie just plain and simple outsmarted you this time."

"He's got you now," Brother Jerry butted in.

Nelson swung his arms wildly in the air to get at Brother Jerry, but Feldstar held him back. Feldstar turned and looked Brother Jerry in the eye.

"Get out of here. Get away from my runner, you mean-spirited son of a— " Feldstar stopped himself. It was the first time Nelson had seen his coach angry.

Feldstar shook himself and turned back to Nelson. "Olie beat you fair and square. He's good. Nothing wrong with that." Feldstar's voice sounded impatient. "Don't let Brother Jerry get to you. Don't let him win. Olie's the challenge. You have two choices. Take it on or let it beat you. What's it going to be, Nelson?"

Feldstar shook Nelson firmly. "Shake it off, buddy! Don't let him win."

Nelson sucked the air into his lungs. *Don't let him win. Don't let him win.* The words ran through his head. It wasn't Olie he had to beat—it was Brother Jerry.

Sister Theresa was so excited about Olie's win that she decided it was time to serve ice cream.

"Children. Children. Children. Attention!" she called. "Time for a break before the final race. Ice cream for everyone is being served at the table."

Nelson drifted away from the crowd and wandered up

to the fence by the woods. He leaned against the fence post, slid down until he was sitting on the grass and looked back at the crowd. Brother Jerry was leaning against the maple. Nelson no longer wanted to beat him up. He felt his anger turn into something else. Determination. Nelson knew what he had to do.

Feldstar brought Nelson a cup of orange juice and sat down beside him. "Here, drink this slowly. You need some energy."

Nelson drank and then stood up. The two walked quietly around the track until Feldstar finally broke the silence.

"What are you going to do, Nelson?"

"I'm going to beat that creep."

"That creep?"

"Yeh—Brother Jerry. The guy who thinks I'm dirt. Well, he's wrong about me, and I'm not going to let him win."

Sister Theresa called the final race. Olie was already waiting when Nelson reached the starting line. This time Nelson took his place to Olie's right.

Feldstar waited at the side. Everyone had entered the cross-country race. There were at least fifteen guys lined up.

"Attention, boys, and listen closely," Feldstar said. "There are orange markers set up along the road. Follow them until you read the sign that says TURN. Sister Madeleine is waiting there for you. Make sure you run around her chair, then head back. Once you get back to the school, you will run four laps around the track to the finish line. Any questions?"

No one said anything, so the runners took their positions.

"Are you ready?"

Nelson looked under the maple. He caught Brother Jerry's eye. The brother glared back at him. His look said, *You are nothing but a loser.*

"GO!"

The gun went off and Nelson quickly took the lead.

Pace yourself. Nelson thought about what Feldstar had said. He turned the corner and headed down West Saanich Road. I *am* paced, he thought. I am in the lead and I am not losing it—not for one stride.

He glanced over his shoulder. Olie was fifteen yards or so behind. He stayed well back, as if he was certain that Nelson couldn't keep up his pace. But Nelson had no intention of slowing down. Instead, he sped up and opened his lead. By the time Nelson reached the TURN sign, Olie was twenty yards behind.

"Good race, Nelson," Sister Madeleine called as he ran around her chair.

Nelson re-entered the schoolyard, looking back down the hill for Olie and the other runners. They were so far behind they were almost out of sight. When the spectators saw Nelson, they erupted into a frenzy. He ignored the ruckus and concentrated on the race. His heart beat, steady and strong. His lungs were clear and fresh. His legs felt light as feathers.

He felt free. Really free.

Olie reached the track as Nelson rounded the first lap. On the second lap, Nelson lifted his head and watched the crowd pass by. Brother Jerry had moved away from the maple and was standing on the sidelines. Nelson looked him straight in the eye as he passed. The brother's face was blank.

When Nelson rounded the final turn of the third lap, the other runners were beginning to enter the track. Sister Theresa and Feldstar unravelled the yellow tape. They each took an end and draped it across after the last runner staggered onto the track. When Nelson saw the tape he got a new burst of energy. He felt like he was a bystander—watching his body perform in a whole new way. He ran as if nothing could stop him. Rosy and the cheerleaders jumped up and down and screamed.

"Nelson! Nelson! Nelson!" The whole crowd joined in.

He swept down the last stretch and lifted the yellow tape high into the air.

Then he turned around and around in joyful glee until he was wrapped in yellow tape like a mummy.

Feldstar picked Nelson up and swung him around. The yellow tape flapped in the wind. The Kuper students crowded around chanting "Nelson! Nelson! Nelson!"

When all the craziness subsided, Feldstar put him down. Nelson unravelled and flopped spread-eagle on the ground, exhausted. Rosy brought him a drink of water, sat down beside him and carefully pinned the blue ribbon onto his sweaty shirt.

"You were incredible, Nelson," she said all aglow. "I have never seen you run like that."

"I won!" Nelson exclaimed. "I beat him!"

"You didn't just beat him, Nelson. He didn't have a chance."

Olie came over, puffing like a deck of smokes, and patted him on the back.

"Great run, cousin. I didn't have a chance."

"Yeh, maybe. But you're a great runner, too."

Nelson looked across the fields. He loved Tsartlip, he realized. And pretty soon he'd be coming back. Kuper Island seemed a long way away now that he was at home. And the sun was shining. And there were eagles, as always, soaring overhead.

Yeh, he thought. I beat him.

But he wasn't thinking about Olie.

About the Authors

Sylvia Olsen (centre) has lived for the past thirty years on the Tsartlip Reserve near Victoria, British Columbia. She became acquainted with Kuper Island Residential School through her mother-in-law and father-in-law, who both attended the school. Over the past decade, Sylvia has studied the effects the school had and continues to have on First Nations individuals and communities. *No Time to Say Goodbye* is Sylvia's first novel. She continues to write and to work as a First Nations community development consultant.

Ann Sam (left) is a member of the Tsartlip First Nation and lives with her family on the Tsartlip Reserve. Along with many members of her family she attended Kuper Island

Residential School. Ann comes from a distinguished family of Cowichan sweater knitters and presently works as a teacher's aide at the Saanich Adult Education Centre.

Rita Morris (right) is a member of the Tsartlip First Nation and lives with her family on the Tsartlip Reserve. Rita's grandparents and some members of her extended family attended Kuper Island Residential School. Rita is currently completing a Bachelor of Education degree at the University of Victoria and intends to pursue a career in education.

About the Illustrator

Connie Paul is a member of the Tsartlip First Nation. She is a registered nurse and an accomplished artist using many media. Connie lives in Nanaimo, British Columbia, with her husband Bill and three sons, Billy, Peter and Brandon. This is Connie's first book illustration.

Also By Sylvia Olsen

The Girl with a Baby

"The perfect daughter in a less-than-perfect family, Jane Williams now has a daughter of her own. ... This is a right-of-passage story, joining the strength and tradition of Jane's [Native] heritage as given to her by her people with her personal struggle to face and win her own battles. This contemporary novel beautifully blends a realistic story of teenage life with a unique view of an old and largely unknown Native culture. This is a common story told uncommonly well."

— *Starred review, School Library Journal*

$9.95 • pb • 1-55039-142-9-X • Teen fiction ages 12+

★ Saskatchewan Young Readers' Snow Willow Award Nominee
★ The Stellar Award: the Teen Readers' Choice Award of B.C. Nominee

White Girl

Fourteen-year-old Josie finds herself living on a reserve outside town, after her mother marries Martin, "a real ponytail Indian," and now she has a new stepfather and stepbrother, and a new name, "Blondie."

"Following her highly acclaimed *Girl with a Baby*, Olsen scores another winner . . . *White Girl* is an outstanding story on may levels, a much-needed addition to the body of contemporary Indian literature for teens."

— *Starred review, School Library Journal*

$9.95 • pb • 1-55039-147-X • Ages 12+

★ Sheila A. Egoff Children's Literature Prize nominee
★ Saskatchewan Young Readers' Choice Snow Willow Award
★ Starred review BOOKLIST

Just Ask Us
A Conversation with First Nations Teenage Moms

Sylvia Olsen takes us behind the "Indian girl with baby" stereotype to enter a conversation with Coast Salish teen mothers and hear first-hand their thoughts on sex, relationships, birth control, abortion, pornography, sex education, self-image, life on the reserve, and much more. Sometimes challenging, sometimes appalling, and always compelling, their stories are essential reading for people in any community who are dealing with teen pregnancy or seeking to better understand why it happens.

$19.95 • pb • 1-55039-152-6 • Non-fiction

Counting on Hope

In the 1850s settlers from Britain began to arrive on Vancouver Island and the surrounding Gulf Islands. Tensions over territory arose between the Coast Salish people and the newcomers. In *Counting on Hope*, Sylvia Olsen tells the story of two girls caught in the middle of the conflict. Letia, a Lemalche girl from Kuper Island and Hope, a British immigrant who lived on a nearby island want to be friends. But their lives are unalterably changed by the turmoil between their people that they cannot control. This book is based on a true story that took place on the Gulf Islands in 1863.

$14.95 – pb – 1-55039-173-9 – Historical Fiction ages 12+

★ City of Victoria Bolen Children's Literature Prize (Winner)
★ Chocolate Lily Award (Nominee)
★ Sheila A. Egoff Children's Literature Prize (Nominee)

Yetsa's Sweater

On a fresh spring day, young Yetsa, her mother and her grandmother gather to prepare sheep fleece. As they clean, wash and dry the fleece, laughter and hard work connect the three generations. Through Yetsa's sensuous experience of each task, the reader joins this family in an old but vibrant tradition: the creation of Cowichan sweaters. Each sweater is unique, and its design tells a story. In *Yetsa's Sweater*, that story is one of love, welcome and pride in a job well done.

PICTURE BOOK • Ages 6–10 • 40 pp
8 x 10 • full colour
$9.95 • paper • 978-1-55039-202-9
$19.95 • hc • 978-1-55039-155-8

★ Shining Willow Award (Nominee)
★ BC Booksellers' Choice Award
  (Nominee)
★ Our Choice (Starred Selection)
★ Silver Birch Express Award (Nominee)

Which Way Should I Go?

Joey is a happy Nuu-Chah-Nulth boy, eager to help and quick to see the bright side of things. But when he loses his beloved grandmother, the sun goes out in his world. Fortunately, she has left something of herself behind—a song, which keeps knocking on Joey's heart, and a dance, which urges him to get up on his feet and choose again. Choosing was what their song was about, and Grandma's lessons prove strong indeed. Joey chooses to remember Grandma with joy and to take up his daily life again with a spring in his step.

PICTURE BOOK • Ages 6–10 • 40 pp
8 x 10 • full colour
$9.95 • paper • ISBN 978-1-55039-214-2
$19.95 • hc • ISBN 978-1-55039-161-9

★ First Nation Communities Read
  Program Selection